Hum
by Ll

Hick Wap Press

HWAP001 / BINGO019
ISBN: 978-1-5272-6264-5

A catalogue record for this book is available from the British
Library.

Cover design by Charlie Kondras
Book design by Charlie Kondras
Printed in Great Britain by CPI Group (UK) Ltd.

Allow a few introductions

Pre-Mortem

I am seated on the couch – against my own wishes – and listening to – no, consuming – the self-absorbed complaints that are being projected orally, from inside somebody's head, through their mouth, towards my face. My hands are bound. Hanging opposite me is a photograph of a malnourished, topless boy. It is black and white and I have seen it before. It was in the bar in Krakow I visited last summer where the barman refused to make recommendations for fear of showing favouritism. The boy is holding his arms up as if crucified.

The lighting is unnecessarily bright – so intense I can feel it. Every now and again my anger ebbs in order to make way for this kind of overwhelming, dizzying nausea. This frustrates me, and I try to fight it off each time, wishing for something more potent – more violent – to fill me up so I might scrape the barrel to find some kind of grit and endurance. Might I faint? Now that would provide some sort of temporary relief, at least.

This is a fucking disaster.

He won't stop complaining. *Apparently* he got laid off, and it's not even his fault. He only missed one shift but the boss had it in for him from the start just because he went to public school. He says the boss had been waiting to give him the boot the whole time he had been there. *Apparently* everything he touches seems to *go to shit* despite his best efforts, and his relationship broke down because the other half – my sympathies are eternally with them – was totally irrational and deliberately sought to cast him in a bad light in an attempt to gain the affections of neutral parties somehow embroiled in the dispute.

Apparently there are not enough varieties of lettuce in the nearest Tesco, so he has to drive thirty minutes to the other one in order to compliment his cheese and ham sandwiches with the correct sort of leaf for each day of the week, because who could possibly survive by just rotating between Chinese leaf and iceberg day in, day out? I tell you, if it wasn't for this ball gag I'd probably be saying something about neurosis, something about priorities and something about the viability of crunchy kale as a substitute.

He makes me want to renounce everything. And nobody is even watching yet.

You see, it's not what he is saying that makes this such a fucking disaster, though that is poor. Nor is it my position. It's his delivery. He is wooden beyond belief. His emotion does not come across in his words. It comes across in my grimaces. Everything he ought to be feeling – or at least pretending to feel – is passed on to me. His anguish becomes mine. His frustration is now my problem. I guess emotion is a constant. It must exist somewhere. And if he won't have it, it seems like I have to make room. He is devoid of all the emotion he ought to have: thus I feel double. I am frustrated that he cannot act frustrated. I am anxious about the poor reception that, in my mind, we will inevitably receive because his anxiety is so utterly unconvincing. I am disappointed that he cannot act disappointed. His inadvertent emotional generosity makes me want to renounce everything. Everything about this job.

That's what it is now: a job. It is now an occupation of emotional violence.

Perhaps I allow things to get to me too much. But then I am a thespian, supposedly. At least I have not yet publicly died. At least, at the moment, my doom is only visible to four people, and two of them are trying to stay positive.

"*It's not surprising. There can't have been a great deal of genuine affection in that relationship; after all that stuff that went on.*"

"*…*"

"*I could tell that must have been the case all along, just from hearing them read the whole sorry tale to us.*"

"*…*"

"*So I'm not surprised he went and did it in the end. It'd been stored up so long, only a matter of time. Only a matter of time really.*"

"*…*"

"*The placid victim, feigning forgiveness for all that time. Allowing the guilt of the other to eventually subside under the false pretence that penance was being paid. The old man felt he was serving with the hope of redemption.*"

"*…*"

"*At least that's how I read it.*"

Olwyn was talking to me about Francis. The man the twelve of us had all been watching. She was helpfully recounting to me all of the information that we had both recently heard coming from the mouth of a gowned stranger.

"*What was it they said? Years of abuse at the hands of his drunken father. Constantly being told he deserved it because he was useless, worthless, unwanted. That's a brutal thing for a child to bear.*"

I allowed her that. Accurate adjective.

"What was the phrase they kept on using? Clutter? Who wants to be told by their own father that they are like some kind of unnecessary junk?"

"…"

"I wouldn't have the patience you know."

"…"

"The patience to wait all that time."

"…"

"You know what I mean? All that time pretending to have forgiven him. Allowing the father to desperately try to make amends by helping him build up that business empire. Giving him all the money he needed. He'd been sober for all thirty of those years, you know. The father."

Of course I knew.

"And then he finally did it. Even though he had ended up with so much. But it was not enough to make him forget. He was still willing to lose it all."

"…"

"Well, I guess he got his revenge."

I shrugged, cocking my head slightly to the right in a gesture of admission.

"At least he allowed his father the luxury of it being painless. If you can go so far as to call it a luxury, that is."

"…"

"Thing is, I'm not sure how he managed to do it. He blindfolded himself? He said, in spite of everything, he still couldn't bear to watch. Really?

9

Do you believe that? How did he find the vein? I suppose elderly people are pretty veiny. They really bulge out sometimes. Maybe he could feel for it."

"…"

Another shrug from me.

"I'm weirdly impressed."

I felt she was allowed to be impressed. I was impressed too.

"Does that make me intelligent in a morbid sort of way, or just stupidly unable to consider the situation without trying to dilute the grim nature of reality with some sort of positivity (however blind) or humour?"

"…"

"Sorry. No pun intended just then."

I hadn't noticed the pun. But there she was with unsolicited attempt at humour again.

"But I feel sorry for him. It's not like he was unprovoked or anything. I think victims ought to be allowed some sort of opportunity to level the playing field, so to speak."

"…"

"At least that's what I think."

"…"

"I couldn't do it though. I couldn't just remove somebody from the world just like that. They don't seem to think he had any previous do they? Maybe we'll find out he did this kind of thing all the time…"

Percussive accompaniment to her voice was provided by a steady drip and a papery rustle coming from somewhere further down the room. The dripping had been a constant, punctuating her sentences with coincidental accuracy the whole time.

A particularly loud drip – one which suggested the plumbing in the room was in a state of swift and unrelenting decline – marked the end of our conversation.

We both stood up, opened our respective doors and went to wash our hands.

I spoke for the first time since we had both entered this section of the building.

"We ought to get back to the courtroom."

Anhedonia Microwave

They looked to be in their early fifties. The man had an air of sophisticated raggedness: overgrown hair and beard offset by a suit well fitted but slightly too short in the leg and the sleeve. The woman who walked alongside him carried herself in a manner which suggested she was the one who had decided where they were going. She walked slightly ahead of her companion – perhaps only by about half a metre or so, but enough to qualify as leader. Their stride was swift and long – purposeful would be an apt description. The woman wore a knee-length sheepskin coat with a woollen collar which she held close around her neck with her left hand. Her tartan scarf flapped behind her head in the brisk wind and she did nothing to restrain its movement. She did not see the point.

They had passed nobody. This was perhaps not too surprising, even though they were walking through the centre of Manchester in the nightclubs' small hours on a Wednesday morning. Just gone kicking out time. They were sticking to back streets. However, even when forced to cross the occasional main road which cut across the woman's pre-planned route not a single other human or vehicle had been present. At some point in the next five minutes they would have to break cover for good and begin to occupy open public spaces, risking being seen at a time in which they really would rather not be seen.

But they were aware of this potential risk and had mentally prepared themselves for it. The man had supposed, out loud, that they were due to perform in one sense or another at some point in their lives. Both of them wore climbing shoes and had covered their hands in chalk dust.

The man pushed his wire-framed glasses up his nose and pointed out to his wife that she ought to do the same. He picked the binoculars from their place resting against his chest and looked up through the opening at the end of the road that had just presented itself as they rounded a sharp corner. They were now in sight of their destination. The woman had registered this slightly ahead of the man and had pulled a pair of compact bolt cutters from inside the deep pocket on the left-hand side of her coat. They looked at one another and smiled.

Next on the agenda was a brisk walk across an open square, deserted except for a couple of street sweepers who were moving away from them, facing the opposite direction. They were pleased by the quietness they encountered. They always preferred to do their business in privacy. They crossed the square in a matter of seconds and found themselves at a wire fence, the panels connected to one another by chains, surrounding what they intended to get to. The woman made a hole with the cutters and pulled the now-loose flap aside for her husband to pass through first. He did so and began to ascend the ramp at the base of their destination, followed closely by his wife who had passed through the fence gracefully moments after him, dropping the bolt cutters as she did so. They clattered onto the floor and she looked back at them briefly before hurrying after her husband.

They were now at the base of Manchester's big wheel. The white framework towered over them as they glanced at each other then directed their gaze heavenwards. The man rubbed his hands together and ran forward, leaping and grabbing one of the white metal bars which made up the structure. His wife did likewise a few feet to his right. They both proceeded to climb expertly, bridging sizable gaps between the girders and moving at a pace likely to turn the stomach of the untrained onlooker. It took them about fifteen minutes to reach the highest point of the wheel, including a brief stop part way up, resting on top of one of the pods, where they reapplied chalk from the supply in the man's inside pocket. Once on top of the highest pod they held hands and looked out over the city.

It really was beautiful. They enjoyed living there. Lights were scattered right the way to the horizon, sporadically interrupting the blanket of blackness, ever so slightly illuminating the areas below. Cars moved beneath them, the perceived volume of this movement reduced by the space between the two atop the wheel and the things they observed. They looked at one another. The woman pushed a sweaty lock of hair out of her husband's eyes and straightened his glasses. The man thanked her and pointed out the street where they had first lived together.

And then they both walked to the edge of the pod and jumped. The man hit white girders as he fell and had nearly completed his task before the point where he landed with a soggy bursting sound. The woman had a clean fall and had crunched to the ground a second earlier. They lay side by side, crumpled up in a pool of blood and exposed innards.

"Are we on air now?"

"Yep… wait… yep, we are on air now."

Hand signals followed. Flattened out palm shaken in front of neck; smiles of assurance; a count down from five, one finger at a time; then a chatterbox – hand-opening-and-closing – motion.

These signals meant nothing to me. I remained mute, holding my face in front of the microphone at exactly the level I had been instructed to hold it. Bill was staring at me, his hand opening and closing repeatedly, his eyes widening, head nodding at some impressive speed. In the end he gave up and asked me a question.

"So, what do you have for us today, Ezra?"

So I wasn't getting any sort of introduction, then. They had announced my presence before the previous song – one of mine – and now seemingly wished to jump straight into it. I felt I needed a little more time. I felt I was being pushed and was worried I would say something I'd come to regret. I continued to receive meaningful looks.

"We really enjoyed the song we just heard; do you have anything to say about it?"

I did not. I had nothing to say about the song. In fact, I had kind of been hoping that the questions would be a little more leading. That he would basically spout off an opinion which I could just reword and reiterate, with a few added pauses to make it sound like I was thinking. These open questions: an interviewer's dream, a (shy) interviewee's nightmare.

"It was on your latest record, right?"

"Yes, it was."

That'll do nicely. Nice and limiting. More of those, please.

"The title track…"

"Indeed it was, that's right, Bill."

I still sounded incredibly halting and uncertain. At least I thought I sounded uncertain. I was certainly answering his questions truthfully, but I was uncertain as to whether the listener could be certain that I was indeed certain that I was telling the truth. I was now certainly over-thinking things. I realised Bill had been talking for a while, filling the listeners in on the information which I was supposed to be providing. Things were evidently coming to a close.

"That was very interesting Ezra. We look forward to your next performances. Thanks for coming on and we hope everything works out for you with this latest record."

"Thanks Bill. See you again."

A song started to play. This time it was not one of mine. Perhaps I had not contributed enough to earn such privilege this time round. My side of the deal had not been fulfilled. So naturally they no longer had any desire to do anything which could be perceived as helpful to me. As if to reinforce this notion they didn't even see me out. A smile and a gesture was all I got now I'd gone and done that. I told myself not to let it bother me.

Bill's younger brother – my flat mate – told me Bill had received a torrent of messages that night commenting on how surly I was. Apparently my public image had suffered a little. I hadn't realised I'd had a public image.

"I wasn't being surly. I was being genuine. I genuinely didn't know what to say."

"Well these guys apparently didn't seem to pick up on your noble genuity."

"Is that the right word?"

"Can you think of anything else?"

I had thought for a bit at that point.

"But then, if I wasn't being genuine – if it was some sort of front I had assumed in the attempt to come across as mysterious or whatever it was I was being accused of – would I be guilty of ingenuity?"

Angus had to think for a while now. He fingered his name badge and thought long and hard.

"Not sure about that one."

"Is it ingenuine… ungenuine… ingenuine? The act of not being genuine is ingenuity?"

"I said I'm not too sure."

"Me neither."

"I'll have a think about it and get back to you."

I had gone to bed that night thinking about whether my unhelpfulness when being questioned by Bill on − − −FM had actually been an unwitting act of ingenuity. Had I been deceiving myself? Had I been deceiving anybody? Had I genuinely wanted to put on a performance of mystique and not even let myself know that that was what I wanted to do? I had been convinced I had not. I had been certain I was much better off being honest and only answering questions I knew I could answer eloquently. Which had turned out to be none of them. Surely there could be no element of ingenuity involved in the act of not speaking simply because you are unable to say anything useful.

Although it now seemed to have backfired, I had felt that my method was a much better approach than to go in with some planned performance – a persona which the media could latch onto and moan about or proclaim an impenetrable genius.

And that last thought – the last few parts of that last thought – made me get out of bed and reach for a dictionary. I spent some time learning the definitions of a couple of words I had previously been misusing. I groaned and smacked the heavy book against my forehead in mock disbelief at my own mistake. But then I thought, perhaps, the meaning I had incorrectly given the word was in fact more appropriate than the offical definition.

Ok, let's get started

<u>Allow me to explain…</u>

I don't even really like acting. My mother used to be scared of the hairdryer. She feared it would melt her hearing aids, and hearing aids were enormously expensive by our standards so she simply thought she couldn't afford to risk drying her hair artificially. You ask why she didn't just take her hearing aids out. Well, that would leave her susceptible to her other, marginally more rational, fear: that she would not hear the bailiffs at the door; would not realise she had to quickly hide; would lose everything. She didn't want us to know about these fears because she felt we needed to see her as unfalteringly strong. So she would often stand in her room, post-shower, and make hairdryer noises so we wouldn't wonder why she never used a hairdryer to dry her hair. Her impressions were incredible. Now that's acting. It didn't last long. I caught her one day when I forgot to knock and ran into her room crying about a stubbed toe. But whilst it lasted it was some serious acting, I'll tell you. So when I was looking for a way to fill my evenings and weekends I thought I'd try it. But it just makes me sort of sad.

Naturally, it makes things worse when somebody acts badly. And that was why yesterday was so fucking awful. Is it still a hobby if you hate it? At least I hate it less than I hate my job. The hobby provides relief in the sense that it is marginally better than what I'd be doing otherwise.

I work as a journalist. I've not been writing much lately, though.

Why am I telling you all this? I'm off on a tangent, aren't I. I've tried to kick this habit – I'm fucking forty now and still unable to explain myself. Come on Jenny. I always had a thing for tangents and meanderings.

Yesterday was awful. Just plain fucking awful. Even the pseudo-optimists gave in eventually. Gave up pretending to be happy. Pretending to give him a chance. I wonder who encourages him to carry on.

I was out and about three days ago. I had been on the phone to Wes for a while, then met Pete and Luce at the pub to chat a bit about work and a lot about nothing. Walking home on my own I popped into a chippy run by a couple. Can't remember the name. I went in – smelt fucking delicious – planning to purchase some chips or something to keep me going on the way home. It was at least a twenty minute walk and I'd had a few and I always get hungry after a few. The thing which struck me about the place had nothing to do with the smell really, though. It was the people.

Back home in Clitheroe, you could count on one thing: Chippy Alan would always be in the chippy. I never wondered why. Never questioned it. It just felt right. Chippy Alan seemed like a guy who you could rely on to be hanging about in the chippy. I am aware that I only formed that impression of

Chippy Alan because the only place I ever saw him was in the chippy. However, my point is this: Chippy Alan was the sort of man you expected to meet in a chippy, so when you did it was no surprise. Sort of anorak-wearing, woolly hat, few teeth missing, rich history. I'm being prejudiced, I know. But I don't sneer at it, I like it. It makes me feel like I am somewhere unpretentious. Somewhere I know.

The people in this particular chippy surprised me so much because of my prejudice.

They were smart, for one. Jackets on most of them, brogues galore. Salt-and-pepper hair flooded the place, flowing in waves from heads sporting wire frames and crow's feet no doubt induced by prolonged squinting. The place sold craft beer, for fuck's sake. I loved it. Androgynous couples stood by the salad stand – an anomaly in its own right in the world of chip shops – discussing things I liked to discuss, but rarely felt able to discuss. All of this is a stereotype, I know. But this is how it happened, I tell you honestly.

Now one thing that is a common factor in all the chip shops I have ever been in is the people behind the counter are the ones who command the undivided attention of people in their near vicinity. This was the case here too. Behind this particular counter there were two people. A man and a woman. The woman wore this fantastic sheepskin coat. I instantly envied her. She commanded the space in which she existed. In one hand she held the chip scoop aloft. The other, with its heavily ringed set of fingers – squeezed into a glove so that the shapes of the stones protruded, almost bursting the straining, fat-glazed latex – spiralled at her ear level as she made her point. The man was stood by the cold tap, holding one of his hands under running water and throwing fish into batter with the other. He was quieter. Jet black, foppish hair fell down onto his face. Whenever this happened the woman's ringed hand would shoot out robotically and brush the lock to one side – she seldom had to look in order to do this, she just did it.

The woman took my order. She seemed quite happy to be working there, despite the hostile hour and the busyness of the place. Once she had taken my order she nodded at the man, who noted it down in two places: first on a scrap of paper shoved onto a nail which protruded above the potato bin, and then into a smart notebook which was placed on a pristine sideboard some way away from the messy cooking area. In the book I saw scrawled paragraphs, along with what were clearly orders and the occasional sketch of a person. There was also a kind of tactical diagram showing a sports team's formation. I didn't ask. As I waited, the woman tried to engage me in conversation. She asked me something about 'authorial intent' but I couldn't confidently answer. I didn't understand. I decided to try anyway, hoping to sound clever, so I told her I thought authors intended to entertain, surely. This seemed to satisfy her in some way, I don't know why. Perhaps she was glad of an answer. My response, I noticed, was not noted down by the man. This is an important point. I then waited for my chips in silence. I was just about the only person there who did not seem to know anybody else.

After about four minutes I got my chips. The woman handed them to me and asked me to wait a second. She then asked me whether authors meant what they wrote. I'm not exactly academic, but even I realised this was basically the same question as the first one, only worded differently. I answered in much the same way, I thought. I told her I believed that authors must mean what they wrote. They were writing to help a reader have a good time. So they must know what they were writing in order to know they were successfully providing a potential reader with a potentially good time, surely? I added the question at the end so that I did not sound too self-assured. Again, the woman smiled. The difference here was that she nodded to the man, who removed his gloves and walked over to the smart book again, turned the page, and started writing something into a three-columned table. I supposed what he was jotting down related to what I had just said. Again, I didn't ask.

Finance

Like most people who write 'musician' in the occupation box on their tax forms, I don't have a lot of money. I mean, I'm not too bad. I'm doing alright. But I'm not doing well enough to be doing it exclusively. So I have a day job. I have a name badge. 'Ezra'. 'Here to help'.

The day job's pretty straightforward. I don't mind the work when it's busy, and Ralph lets me write stuff when it's quiet. I keep a guitar behind the desk so I can mess about on that when I have a spare minute. Ralph's a good boss. He heard my interview. He said it was ingenious and then he smirked. Did he know?

Nine quid an hour. And if I sell anything from The Shelf I get half the money as some sort of commission. It's an arrangement Ralph has never explained but I'm not complaining. It keeps me going. And I supplement it with what I make from the vocation. But that tends to get spent on tour anyway – I'm not grown up enough yet to squirrel any of my money away, I'll be the first to admit.

The place is a bloody tip. Ramshackle shelves everywhere, propping up their wares just barely. It's fucking great. There are literally thousands; tens of thousands of books. All second hand, often rag-tag, always with a story – no pun intended. If I don't want to write I can just read. Ralph does a pretty good business with the hip contingent round here in Manchester. A few of my mates come in, if you'll allow me to insinuate that I am part of said contingent. I'll allow myself a few flattering remarks, I think. The room is massive. I can't see the far end from where I am sat because higgledy piggledy shelves go all the way up to the ceiling at times. At the centre of the shop there is a spiral of shelves which manifests a sort of maze with a little clearing at the centre. Ralph is very much the idiosyncratic shelf-arranger. There are trinkets everywhere. In the spaces between books there are random articles of Ralph's own possession. Shop protocol is you can touch and move, but don't fucking nick anything. And people respect that.

The exciting thing is that I basically run the place at the moment. Ralph still controls it, but I run it. Ralph's busy on a new project. This project started last year but is only just beginning to be taken even vaguely seriously by outside parties. 'Song Street Publishing Arm'. Sounds interesting, right?

Backwards, With Progress

"Is that woman outside again?"

The man was peering out of the window; the outside was so dark that his black hair merged with the black square through which he looked.

"I can't see." He put his hands on either side of his face like blinkers and squinted harder. His wife moved over towards him in the dark room and gathered the curtains around his neck, so as to prevent any stray light from revealing his face to the outside.

"I'm pretty sure that we're clear."

"Good."

"I haven't seen her for a while. I think she was probably harmless."

"Still…"

"You're right. We don't want her to watch this."

They drew the heavy curtains closed, taking care not to displace the cloth that was placed over the curtain rail to prevent light escaping through any gap above it. They double checked that the two drapes crossed one another in the centre, sealing off the outside altogether. All was well. The woman moved across the room and switched on the light.

"Must we do this? We could always go somewhere else, far away, and start again."

"Like where?"

"I don't know. My parents' would love to have us back, I'm sure."

"You want us to run away to Sri Lanka – where neither of us have lived since we were teenagers – and move in with your parents?"

"I don't know."

"Home's been here for more than three decades now. Summer holidays back there, so close to both our families, are hard enough."

They both smiled and no audible answer was given. The man sat down and removed his wire-framed glasses for a moment. He fingered the edge of the chair's arm and stared at the ground. They both remained silent for a while.

"What do you think she wanted?"

"..."

"Did she even want anything from us? She never actually opened her mouth. Just looked from side to side. Then she ran off."

"..."

"Interesting."

"There must've been something in it. She didn't seem..."

"But how can you tell?"

"I'm not sure."

Silence resumed, except for the irregular ticking from the clock in the hall that needed its batteries changing. The woman's facial expressions made it clear that she found this severely irritating, but was unwilling to solve the issue herself. There was no point, now. She reached for the coat rack to her left and plucked from it a long tartan scarf. She

31

wrapped it around her neck and tucked the ends into her zipped-up coat. She made eye contact with her husband and jerked her head towards the door.

"You've got your shoes on?"

The man got up and laced up a pair of shoes she had left waiting for him on the coffee table.

"Yes."

"Then let's go."

"Yes."

The man sat back down again.

She left the room for a moment and feet moving up stairs caused a dull thud, permeating throughout the house and rousing the man from his reverie. He looked up from the floor, stood up and walked out of the room. He headed towards the front door.

When she came back down stairs the man was slumped against the door, his eyes unblinking, head lolling forward in defeat.

"What?"

He mumbled, his mouth buried deep within the thick collar of his overcoat, which had risen up towards his head. He looked like a tortoise mid-retreat.

"The fucking door's jammed."

The woman looked above her husband's head at the door. The key protruded from the lock, twisted about ninety degrees so that the circular part at the end was parallel with the ground and the ceiling. The door handle pointed downwards.

"Let me try."

"You can try, but it's jammed."

"I'll try. I bet it's not jammed really."

"You can try, but I assure you that it is jammed. Check yourself for peace of mind if you wish."

"By the way, did you lock up the shop?"

"We left it for dead. Gave up. You said you didn't see the point."

"I know but there are sharp things in there. People could take them. And use them."

"No, I didn't lock it. But who cares? Focus on this door. Try the door."

She tried the door. After a few wrenches she gave up. The man then stood up and went to the cupboard under the stairs. His top half momentarily disappeared as he reached in, then came back into view. In his left hand was a hatchet. Its weight caused his shoulder to droop as he carried it. As he walked the axe bumped noisily against bulging, metallic pockets.

"I suppose it doesn't really matter now…" the woman muttered. "Go ahead."

She moved back, out of the way.

A splintering sound and not much visible progress to go with it. The man reached in and pulled a few splinters away.

"Fuck."

"What?"

"Got a splinter."

"Oh really."

"Yeah."

He tried again, swinging more heavily this time, so much so that the woman instinctively ducked despite being some distance behind him. The jagged scar in the door widened. He went again. And once more. By the fifth swing there was a decent sized hole, about waist height.

"What if somebody thinks we're being burgled and comes out to look?"

A good point. The hole was the size of a snakes and ladders board. The man looked through it.

"Grab my legs"

"Why?"

"Feed me through. Like a letter."

She did. The jagged edges of the hole snagged his shirt, so he used the axe to give them a trim before his wife followed him through. She then leaned into the hole and held her arms out for the man. He held her by the wrists and pulled her out into the front garden. No lights in the neighbours' windows. No attention yet.

They brushed themselves off, removing nothing from their bodies, performing the action out of habit more than anything else. They both looked down the garden path together, out onto the dimly lit road on which they lived.

"Okay. Let's go," she said.

Midday Booksellers

The shop was dead. Feet on the edge of the desk. Don't rock on your chair. Everybody's heard about that kid who rocked on his chair, fell back and smacked his head on a ledge just like that one you're sat in front of. You could see the bone of his skull, the cut was that deep.

One person poked their head up and asked if they still had that 1930s leather bound fuck-off massive collected works of Bernard Shaw. The person's words.

They didn't. The person left. The clock in an unseen corner chimed twelve times. It was annoying. Ezra closed his eyes and tilted his head back. To say he fell asleep would be inaccurate. Time moved fast, as it often did when Ezra wanted it to. Possessed with some sort of near-impossible ability to defy the old adage that referenced the aerial ability of time during moments of pleasure, Ezra found it remarkably easy to allow work to pass by, as long as he didn't have to understand or control anything. The flip side of this ability was, of course, the frequent difficulty encountered when roused from this state that he so often allowed himself to slip into.

The intrusion of a person startled the semi-supine Ezra into kicking against the desk and knocking his precariously balanced chair out from under him. He fell, hitting his head on a bookshelf. He got up and checked for any exposed skull.

Ralph was back. Ezra tried to remember things about him so as to facilitate some sort of small talk.

"How's the publishing side of things going?"

"Alright thanks. Got a couple of writers I'm interested in. Thanks for your help and all this."

"No worries. Up to much now?"

"Not really, just dropping by to check in."

"All's fine boss. Quiet day."

"As ever."

"Unfortunately yes."

"Fair enough. Okay, I'd better move along again. Thought I'd meet one of these authors over a pint and have a chat. See what they think."

"Thought you said you hadn't much on?"

"That was in that exact moment. I'm specific with my time, you know that."

"I do."

"Ta ta."

He was gone before Ezra could answer.

Ezra walked over to the single bookcase that covered one of the walls of the office – if you could decorate such a room with a term like office, which seemed to lend the place an undeserved association with professionalism – and took out a book. He flicked to the end to check if anything interesting was going to happen, scanning over the final two chapters. He decided that the book wasn't for him and put it back down. Ralph encouraged the impossibility of his staff reading all of the books that the shop had on offer. There were thousands and

Ezra had read somewhere that if you wanted to write, you had to avoid reading fiction. Something about it all being lies, anyway. Worst case scenario he could just tell the hypothetical inquisitive punter how the story ended and let them read the book to see how it got there.

As if the day had barely happened Ezra found himself outside the shop turning the key in the lock of the front door. Time had breezed by. Total takings: seventy-three pounds, and most of that was from online transactions. Ezra didn't remember checking but the crumpled piece of paper with the figures on it was in his left pocket. He'd better email that information to Ralph when he got home. Anything on tonight?

Nope.

A dull one. Hopefully that'd go by quickly as well. Skip on to the good bits, that's what he reckoned.

<u>Reading Electronic Devices:</u>

I am on a train and in my hands there is a book. I'm tired and I can feel the congealed mass of last night's takeaway nestling somewhere around my abdomen. At least I think that's what that heavy feeling is. Next to me there is a man who makes me want to get to know him well enough that I notice when he has died. I will then revisit my old, short-lived career as a registrar and have the satisfaction of registering his death – officially terminating his existence. He's using an eReader. He's reading something appalling.

His face is glossy and induces sexual despair. I am in the window seat and the ticket above his seat says that he too is here all the fucking way to Clitheroe. I am trapped. I might order a coffee and spill it on him. I can hear the rattle of the trolley making its way towards us – why are we an 'us' now? I fiddle around for some change and touch his thigh. He looks up and grimaces, but I think it is a grin. I try to burp so I can compare the inevitable grimace that would cause to what I just saw him do. I hope I do not also induce sexual despair. Well, in him, maybe. But not in general. I'm only fucking forty.

I'm visiting my dad in his care home. He's seventy now and he's a pervert. I don't want to visit, but at least it'll be short and I can be back in town this evening. The only thing keeping me going – and I know that this will sound extremely strange – but the only thing that is keeping me going is the hope that I will run into the owners of that chip shop in a different context at some point. I want to know them. I wonder how I can manufacture that.

Twenty minutes to go.

My father lives in a place called Prickle Manor. It's nice, but he doesn't really need to be in a care home in my opinion. He had an alcohol-induced stroke about ten years ago and had a girl who came and checked up on him for a few years. Then they slept together – which was really fucking weird – and she got sacked. So he started drinking again and now he's in this home so somebody else can be responsible for him rather than having him being responsible for himself. In my pocket is three-hundred millilitres of Polish absinthe.

Glossy-face struggles up and this suggests that we have arrived, or that he is popping off to use the toilet before the train stops. I especially despise people who obey the 'no-use-whilst-stationary' rule in train lavatories. No, he's getting off.

My father models himself on Richard Brautigan. Look him up. He's a counter-cultural author from the 60s. Beautifully moustachioed, often ponchoed, usually behatted. I'm doing that thing I often do where I speak about a relatively well-known cultural figure as if they are my own personal secret. You probably know who he is.

Anyway, today my father's Brautiganesque, Custeresque moustache is flecked with strawberry yoghurt. I slip him the drink and he thanks me. Week: fine. Happenings: nowt. Myself: not much either. Plans: none. Work: 'fraid not, Dad. Why: disillusioned. Why: last time was shit. New plans: what like? Write something: Maybe. Something you choose to write yourself, not a commission; you were quite good last time I saw: Yeah, maybe. Yeah, perhaps more than maybe. I suppose I'd need to write something so I could pay my rent. May as well be about something that interested me. Or I could work in a bar. Or rely on handouts. You're right. I need more ambition.

I'll live within my means. I'll scrounge and write, just like every twat I slept with at university said he would. Fuck, I'm regressing.

Dad was drunk by the time I left. Blimey, he necked that. I'll have to sneak him more next time. His hands shook badly the whole time I was there but I ignored this. Well, obviously I didn't. We had moved from the lounge back into his room and listened to some of his records. Mainly spoken word, with some independent Australian bands thrown into the mix. Quite eclectic, I'll say. His room is decorated with fishing paraphernalia, although he never fished himself. Not his real self anyway.

I left inspired.

Drawing

In the pristine room on the first floor of the head offices of Chocofix Corp. a man in an unnecessary lab coat and an apron perched in front of an easel, on which sat a large plywood board, stapled to which was the smallest canvas that he'd ever worked on. It was stapled exactly to the middle of the board, occupying a space of about three centimetres squared. Dimensions and intricacies were essential here. What he was drawing had to be greatly detailed. It needed to survive the scrutiny of the magnifying lenses through which it would be viewed by hundreds and hundreds of people who had just woken up, tearing open the orange wrapper, trying to brighten up their breakfast with a brief glimpse of something that was anything but the morning that faced them.

That being the hard sell he had been given by the boss, the artist was a little put out by the nature of what it was that he was drawing. Given the aforementioned pitch, he had been expecting something idealistic, perhaps something vaguely trippy – something as far removed from the horrors of reality as he could feasibly dream up in his well-exercised imagination. But sadly – in a move that contradicted significant elements of the boss' usual laissez-faire leadership policy – the artist had been commissioned with a specific set of drawings that he needed to create for the latest set of free gifts.

He was using a really, really thin pen to do this.

He was struggling to work out how he would make it look like the people were falling, rather than flying. Apparently this was important. He had them, viewed from the back, hand in hand but starting to pull apart, mid-air. Their coats were flapping behind them, scarves autonomous, hair doing what it liked. He had opted for a near-birds-eye view, done just so that you got a glimpse of what it was that they had leapt from. He hadn't got round to drawing that bit yet – he wanted to try and keep that subtle. Perhaps just a bit of white in the corner, and a tell-tale shadow barely distinguishable on the floor, caused by streetlight. This was the bit of the drawing that he was really interested in. Not that he'd ever be told why this had been asked for. But it was what they were supposed to have jumped from that was just a bit *weird*.

The two of them entered the room without knocking. He had invited them. He felt that it was about the right time to do this. The musical one had been working there for quite a while so it seemed a worthwhile investment to show him how things operated round the back. And the other – the longish-haired, fattish one – worked on the radio and that interested Ralph.

Ralph heard them walk to the centre of the room. He had emptied it the day before. All its contents were now in storage about half a mile away. A puzzled noise. Then somebody – the grunting suggested perhaps Bill – squatted down and started to undo the zip.

"Ralph, why are you inside a tent?"

Ralph did not answer. He looked up from his book and stared into their faces. They took this for an answer nonetheless and came inside. They sat down on the prepared cushions.

"Hi."

"Hi Ralph."

They looked around them, almost in unison. In the centre of the tent was a pole which held the roof up. Attached to this pole was a series of photographs. At the top pole was a picture of a note on which, in Ralph's sloping handwriting, there was written the word 'targets'.

The tent was sort-of-circular, and would have

been significantly more so had it not been erected in such a hasty manner.

"Welcome to Song Street Publishing Arm HQ."

"Oh, wow. It's nice."

"I'll do all of my business inside this tent, I think. It keeps it separate from the shop, but still linked in a way, too."

"That it does. I agree."

"Drink?"

"Go on."

Ralph reached towards the other item in the room: a crate filled with bottles of cider.

"Made this."

"You did?"

"Yes."

"Cheers Ralph."

Ralph turned to Bill. Bill was a man of the world – a man with a bona-fide white collar job.

"Is this a gimmick, Bill?"

"Is what a gimmick?"

"This, what I'm doing now. The tent."

"Well, not especially." A long pause; then, bashfully: "Yes."

"Thought so. That's good. If somebody like you thinks it is a gimmick then I suppose the people I am trying to attract will think it is marvellous. Ezra, do you like it?"

"I think its fucking marvellous," Ezra replied, grinning.

"Case in point."

They all nodded.

"Do the zip back up will you."

Somebody could be heard entering the shop in the other room. Ralph waved his hand dismissively when Ezra and Bill looked towards him, seeking acknowledgement.

"Actually Ralph, we thought that we might ask you a question." Bill was speaking.

"Go on."

"Did you hear that interview I did with Ezra about his latest record?"

"No."

"OK. Well, still, the question is something you might answer, we think."

"Go on."

"Right, well it was after the interview and Ezra and my brother had a chat about the whole thing. Just to fill you in, I got a lot of texts in..."

"Texts in to what?"

"The radio programme."

"People can text radio programmes?"

"Well, they text me and I read out what they say, provided it isn't telling me to go fuck myself or anything..."

"Go and fuck yourself." Ralph smiled.

Bill watched.

"Anyway, lots of people texted in saying Ezra wasn't open enough. They felt he didn't really engage. They felt that he was trying to be mysterious and was not behaving in a genuine manner."

"But I just didn't want to say stupid things. I just didn't know what to say so I kept my mouth shut."

"Which I think is fair."

"But was I, by doing that, being ingenuine?"

"Ingenuine is not a word, Ezra."

Ezra paused.

"Oh. Right."

They all looked at one another. Ezra turned to his left.

"I told you, Bill."

"What?" Slightly affronted.

"I told you. I looked it up in the dictionary."

"I wanted to check."

"Let's leave this now."

Manifesto

Bill had gone and Ezra had stayed. They were back to talking about Ralph's new project.

"It needs work, Ralph. It's not quite there yet."

"I know that." Ralph looked down, obviously stung. Ezra realised his mistake.

"But I think you're onto something here. Something like this could be really good for young writers. And you could give away free samples of new stuff with books you sell in the shop. You're your own means of promotion to other book lovers."

Ralph looked riddled with self-doubt; a faux-thoughtful pout upon his mouth and a slight, involuntary shake of the head as soon as Ezra informed him that he was 'onto something here.' Ezra grew frustrated. He composed himself and began to compile in his mind a way in which he could rectify the damage that his passing criticism seemed to have caused. He was not going to enjoy this.

Ezra began to talk and ceased to be really aware of what it was that he was saying. Following some sort of subconsciously settled-upon strategy of combining compliments with vague claims of experience, Ezra started to talk Ralph down from his ideological precipice. He wished he could do this more often – in job interviews perhaps. To be able to, on demand, detach himself from what he was saying, so that it slid by in a way that he didn't feel, but still be secure in the knowledge that the shit he was spouting was exactly what the other people wanted to hear. A subconscious filter that knew what to say and when, if only his conscious self would just take a step back and just *shut the fuck up.*

Ralph looked at Ezra. Ezra felt like he had done nothing.

"Fine. You've convinced me."

Ezra left the shop a few minutes later, aware that he had done something morally ambiguous, but not sure what. Now alone with his thoughts, he wondered if he had developed a means by which he could suppress his conscience when bored – the ability to zone out without feeling the need to express his dissatisfaction with circumstance. Maturity, perhaps. He smiled inwardly and started to walk home. He stuck his headphones in. A song about the impossibility of ever being truly satisfied in the time which immediately follows a fresh haircut.

Rejection Note

Dear Mr and Mrs —,

I hope you appreciate the fact that I have taken the time to contact you, especially given that I have been rather busy of late.

My feedback is as follows: I believe that your book is shit. And I believe that deep down, perhaps somewhere within you both that is as of yet unexplored, you share my opinion. I genuinely do.

Thank you,
Rev. Ralphonse Ralfonso

"Ralphonse?"

"Prick."

"Well, I guess that's it then."

She folded the letter back into its envelope and put it on the table. She looked at it and then looked away, promising herself she wouldn't look at it again.

It was this occasion that cemented within the man's mind the association between the smell of honey and abject failure. These two things would remain associated, in his head, for the rest of his life. His wife had not spoken since her utterance of the obscenity; she continued to spread honey on her toast as if he had just read out a reasonably boring local headline.

The clock on the wall told him that it was mid-morning, but it may as well have been dark. He stood up, pushed his chair back from the breakfast table and moved over to the window. In attempting to draw the curtains – thus blocking out the inappropriately uplifting morning sunlight – he knocked a dish off the drying rack. Rather suitably, it broke and he left the pieces on the floor. Still, the woman did not look up from her now glistening toast. The viscous spread was running down the slope at which her hand was tilting the bread and threatening to drip onto the floor and join the fragments of crockery in their state of dejected terrestrial disarray. The man imagined this Ralphonse slipping on spilled honey and landing on fragments of crockery, putting his back out and perforating his perfect porcelain skin; but that wasn't nearly painful enough.

The woman finally looked up. She looked blank – pointedly blank. Then she spoke.

"I don't see the point in going back to work again, then."

"Me neither."

"Shall we shut it up?"

"Just leave it. It doesn't matter."

They both glanced over at the window.

"Open the curtains. Why did you shut the curtains?"

The man moved back over to the window, careful to avoid the broken dish and the honey, which had indeed followed its projected course.

He dragged the curtains apart.

"It's nice to let in a bit of sunlight. Wakes you up."

"Yeah. Wakes you up to news like this. Great."

The man sat back down again. He stared into his half-eaten bowl of cereal. Next to his left wrist was the complimentary toy that had come with the packet. Chocofix. Whole-grain, chocolaty religious symbols. He picked up the free gift and pulled apart the opaque orange cellophane wrapper. Inside was a miniature version of the children's ViewMaster toys. The type where you looked through the goggles at one end and inside there was a 3D picture. The proper versions came with wheels, where at regular intervals there featured a different image that you could view if you turned the disc. Irritatingly, this cheap version had no wheel. The picture was fixed. You looked through the lenses and there you had it. Your only option. The accompanying leaflet encouraged the man to collect them all, and then, when stared into in a certain order, a story would be revealed picture by picture. They appeared to be numbered so as to aid you in viewing them in the right order. There were five in the series. The man's was labelled with the number four. He held it up to his eyes and peered into it. The picture inside was of a Ferris wheel.

"What are you doing?"

"Looking at this free toy thing."

"We got another one? Anything interesting?"

He did not reply. They resumed silence for a period of time. The woman was not necessarily trying to start a conversation when she said:

"What do we do now?"

Further Investigations

Jenny was stood at the bus stop, feeling like she was overreacting to last night's self-assured TV meteorology. She had decided. She was heading back to the chip shop. But this time in the daytime. She had thought rain, it had spat a little, it was now hot. But to remove her jumper would be to reveal her accidental pairing of navy with black – and neither was denim.

A bus arrived but she decided against it. She would walk. It wasn't far, really. The route had a lot of densely located stops, which usually made the ride feel longer than it actually was.

The bus ambled past, coughing dirt at her as if to say it didn't want her anyway. She felt reassured by this, interpreting it as symbol of mutual disdain, then realised she was being ridiculous, then walked.

She had walked it the other night. Remarkable what sobriety can do to your confidence in your physical resilience. The chip shop was in a low-rise part of Manchester, on the outskirts. From here you could see the chimneys in the city centre, protruding above the flat-roof pubs and small, pseudo-professional office complexes further out. Both were already occupied, with varying degrees of misery being provoked within Jenny as a consequence.

She wondered why they had picked this place. It couldn't have had too much footfall. Then again, if the chips were as good as she remembered, perhaps they attracted the customers. She located the shop at the end of the road onto which she had just turned. She saw that it had a title. Or a name. Title seemed appropriate, somehow. It grew as she approached it, as if asserting itself.

Wooockip

Woodckip... woodsomething – whatwasthat?

Woodchips: there we are

Wood Chips

Wood Chips

WOOD CHIPS (OK, I've got it, alright.)

She was at the front door. The sign read 'Open'. She tried the door and entered.

Nobody was there. Not even behind the counter. She decided to have a look around. What was the name about? That was shit. It was a shit name.

The vats were piping. There was an absurd air of activity to the place, despite it being completely empty. She shouted a brief greeting and, as expected, received no reply.

There was a notice, pinned to a board next to many others. It read as follows:

Dear customers,

We hope you are well. We are out. However, contrary to the advice of the Fire Brigade, we have left the chip pans on. Feel free to pop behind the counter, chuck a few potatoes in from the barrel and serve yourself. We don't really mind all that much about payment. Consider this portion on us!

We ask only one thing. Please write, in the notebook below this notice, the exact number of chips you have taken, along with the name of your favourite record, holiday destination, TV programme; whatever really. Take the opportunity to recommend to us something you deem unmissable!

Regards,
The owners.

Jenny looked down at the book. It was the one she had seen the man behind the counter using the other day. The page at which it was left open already contained a number of entries. Hugh had taken thirty-six chips and liked a band he said was from Leeds. Dorothy had only taken ten as she didn't want to be cheeky, and informed them that the latest series of a popular TV show about a mixture of posh and poor people in the olden days had her absolutely addicted. Tom said he was taking a rough guess at forty, and said he missed that children's TV series where parents got gunged for committing staggeringly minor misdemeanours, whatever it was called. There were a few more. Behind the leaf on the left-hand side of the open double page were many slightly crumpled, assumedly filled-in pages. The papers that made up the smaller pile of pages behind the leaf on the right-hand side were pristine.

Whiter. Virginal, supposedly. Jenny decided to have a rifle through the crumpled section. She checked behind her. There was nobody at the door.

The first thing she came to was a page full of doodles. They were caricatures, perhaps of the people who came to the chip shop. She opened up another random page – quite near to the one at which the book had originally been left open. This was the table she had seen being filled in the other night. She glanced at it. It was full of data – the first column contained brief descriptions of people. Rough age, accent, names if they had them, miscellaneous details that had been picked up in brief, over-the-counter conversation; the latter two of the columns housed the recording of a number of answers to various questions, including the ones she had been asked when she last visited. The first of these two columns was labelled 'before order: assumedly hungry' and the second was labelled 'after service: placated (hopefully)'. Jenny's answers were there, among the others. She turned back to the page where the book had been left open.

Zero, lost my appetite. Big fan of Estonia, Hungary – that vague area. Cheap too.

She left with the resolve to look into these people further; the people who ran this shop and recorded this data. Interesting characters, Jenny suspected. The sort she needed to investigate if she was to successfully act upon her father's suggestions.

A tall, red brick cuboid with somebody inside it

Sometimes I feel like I have no control over my own life. I know what you are thinking. All I do is work in a bookshop and piss about on my guitar. What is there to lose control over? But that's how I feel.

Not in a sort of pseudo-sexy chaotic look-at-me-I'm-so-wild sort of way. In a holy-fuck-this-is-annoying sort of way. It's like zoning out, and I snap back into the present after unfeasible amounts of time have gone by. I feel like I've missed out. Sometimes it's quite nice. At first I was excited by it. I thought it was like skipping to the good bits. But I've learned. Often it's a nightmare. I come back and only hope I haven't hit somebody with a golf club or drowned somebody in a bath. Or, I guess more likely, forgotten to go to the toilet and pissed myself, or something.

I think I'm noticing a pattern in it all. I'll explain it properly when I'm sure. I don't want to speak too soon. At the moment it's vague, and could prove to be total bullshit. So far there's not enough evidence to really establish a hypothesis, so let's call it a pre-emptive supposition. If that makes any sense. It'd only take one or two anomalies for me to go back to believing things are normal. That I'm just being paranoid.

But for now, let's agree this is true. Humour me, at least.

Yesterday I had some errands to run. Or rather, Ralph had some errands to run. As his subordinate, this meant that the errands became, in part, mine as well. The reason was that he had this massive box of books he needed carrying somewhere, and it was much easier to carry if there were two of us. He wouldn't tell me why the books needed moving. Naturally, I helped him out. Ralph didn't worry about closing the shop during business hours because he isn't the most business-minded of people. He said he figured we wouldn't lose much custom that day, anyway. I must say, I was a little put out. I'd still get my wage, but it ruled out any chance I had of selling something from The Shelf that day. Nevertheless, I could hardly refuse, could I? He's my boss. Neither of us drive. That fact may answer a few outstanding questions you may have as a result of my convoluted and ill-sequenced story.

So there we were, staggering up Song Street with this fuck-off massive box full of copies of a thick hardback. I don't know if the book was really good or something, but the amount of copies we were carrying far outstripped the level of demand there could be for anything we typically sold, as far as I was concerned. Perhaps I exaggerate, but you must bear in mind I spent a day lugging books around. And that wasn't even the most taxing part of the debacle. We were walking down Song Street with this massive box of thick books, grunting by way of complaint regarding our situation. It was a good twenty minutes at normal walking pace to Ralph's mum's – that was where we were headed – and would take us probably about three hours at this rate, with this burden. We were not happy.

Ralph's phone – I never had him down as a phone owner – rang. I told him I never had him down as a phone owner and told him that he must give me his number, for the sake of practicality more than anything. He said it was a work phone.

And then I have no memory for a while. I hadn't been drinking, but I sort of zoned out.

It began as soon as it became obvious that Ralph's conversation was going to be a lengthy one, and next thing I knew we were at the door of this industrial looking complex of buildings on the outskirts of town. I had realised upon looking in my wallet that I was a bus fare down, and the box of books was gone. I asked Ralph what had happened and he looked at me and listed a number of occurrences I was not aware had taken place. The news was not good. Ralph informed me that we were in his mother's bad books, as we had received a phone call demanding our presence at wherever it was that we had travelled to, and as a consequence we'd had to get rid of the books as quickly as possible. Naturally, that meant Ralph rang his mother, who'd had to leave the vegetables on a low heat and drive out quickly to come and pick up the box, which her son forbade her from opening. For some ludicrous reason she must've obeyed him.

He rattled it off like that. Matter of fact, glossing over the supposedly irrelevant minutiae. Yet while all that he described was actually happening I hadn't noticed any of it. I had just shot through it all. And here's the weirdest thing about it. Ralph never mentioned me blacking out. He seemed to think I'd been functional the whole time. Now, you know I am at times proud of my ability to zone out and seemingly pass through time when I am bored. But I would much rather I was in the driving seat when I was doing it.

I have two issues with it happening of its own accord. One: no control. What if my brain has a different taste in what is interesting to the rest of me? Two: the fast-forwarding itself means the bit that was uninteresting is now interesting. Fast-forwarding through time is undoubtedly interesting. Sort of self-defeating, it seems. Well, three issues. Three: it's fucking weird and I'd rather this sort of thing remained within the world of fiction. And hang on, four: what if it happens again? Or, what if it never happens again, and I stop being certain that it ever happened in the first place?

I need a lie down. Maybe Ralph's given me something.

I may as well explain what happened next, though, since I can remember that bit. I'll try to explain what this factory business of Ralph's was all about. How accurately I can do that, I don't know. At the time I was still reeling from my recent uncertainty over my own ability to understand what goes on both in and outside of my head.

You know the standard, over-sentimentalised, red brick nonsense that people from Manchester often harp on about: coming home to see the chimneys rising up on the horizon like a big middle finger gradually being erected in semi-hostile greeting. Well it was sort of like that, but focus on the middle finger bit and steer clear from the sentimental stuff. An air of hostility is what we're aiming for. The place was unwelcoming.

Dirt-stained brickwork – iconic to the area yet present in such quantity that individual cases mean nothing. The whole building emanated nothingness. And we walked straight in.

The first thing I noticed about him was that he was so robotic that it was transfixing. Efficiency – certainty – condensed into something sort of sexual. For a moment I refused to believe in him. This suspension of belief became impossible when he started to speak, and he did so articulately.

I cannot replicate what he said. I am too scared to do that. Everything felt so covert.

Ralph's reply was reluctantly positive. I don't know if there was money in it or anything like that. I was then led back outside and we took the next bus back towards the centre of town. I slept in the tent that night.

<u>This is getting a bit wanky now.</u>

He was hunched, expensive suit jacket hooked onto the edge of wingback, low card table out in front, screen propped up in front, staring intently. He probably thought he was bohemian, hand in lap and active.

The room was large and sparsely furnished, the untreated wooden floor creaked with almost every jerk due to the slightrock suffered by the chair as a result of an uneven leg, near-negligible wisps of light struggling through one grimy window, an attic above a warehouse or something, one supposes.

This was work, technically. The threat of this not working out was more than just a threat to his basic desire to experience the luxury of pleasure at all times. It was a threat to his livelihood. So ensuring success was valuable work.

He needed things done, and he was stressed about that. Everybody needs a break sometimes. Downtime is as important as graft: it means you can fire on all cylinders when that is required. The anxiety he felt was only on the fringes of his consciousness when he was engaged in this manner – fixated on the best outcome possible – the idea that everything could work – tangible eroticism in a metropolis of discontent, made possible by capitalist success and the mortality of the perceived good idea. He wanted it done meticulously – it would be pointless if it wasn't done this way.

He finished, smudged off button pressed, no result. The screen was frozen. On it was an image of a human form, suspended mid-air, in front of an out-of-focus roller coaster.

Note to cleaner to sort the splattering out in the morning. A joke: might need an ice scraper.

A head popped around the door – made an address to Mr Crampian – the taxi had arrived. Home time. It took a few minutes to get to the car and then it slid, past dirty brick industrial buildings and off to wherever the rich live.

Curtail

The pair of them left the bookshop having dropped off their package.

The friendly world of yet-to-be-achieved success. The sense of potential somehow satisfies; somehow occupies the mind completely yet still, ultimately, qualifies as distraction. Some would call it hope. Everything rested upon it, but not enough time had elapsed since its conception for its intangible flimsiness to have dawned upon them. They had already decided on a contingency plan, but for now that was not even relevant. For now, hope was relevant.

The tent had smelled like burnt toast; the man appeared to have been living almost exclusively within it. A small gas stove was being dangerously utilised within the canvas confines. The zip opening had been hurriedly resealed as soon as they had entered bearing their stack of paper. He had sat there and stared at them until they were uncomfortable.

"Will you?"

"I'll take a look."

"..."

"No promises."

"..."

"Don't get your hopes up."

"We will not."

And then they had left.

There was a fair spring to their step. The cracked pavement beneath their feet seemed to close in on them and then recede. They walked quickly, planning to go out for a celebratory breakfast. They had finished their project. They had sent it to the person they believed it was necessary to send it to. It was now out of their hands. They felt unburdened. Hence the celebration: a rare luxury in their lives.

They were well aware of the apparent lack of viability of the group to which they had submitted their precious work. The calculated lack of organisation and the meticulous quirk did not exactly bode well if one's interpretation of boding well relied on the belief that things would be carefully managed, professional and, most of all, genuine. However, what enabled their present positive outlook was the hope that if it did work out well, then it would be gloriously artful. They were completely aware of the inevitable accusations of pretentiousness – something that would come regardless of their success or failure – yet, in a way that actually made them rather embarrassed about themselves, this reaffirmed their belief in what that they were doing. They walked breakfastwards.

They rounded a corner, moving onto a street containing a number of the sort of cafes commonly found near to independent bookshops. No doubt the patrons of the former would perch alfresco, second-hand copies of famously difficult books purchased from the latter resting conspicuously on their laps as they sipped drinks they did not like to drink with names they did not like to pronounce, in both cases due to a deep fear of doing it wrong. The couple walked up the street, not knowing where they wanted to go but knowing for certain where they did not want to go. The average onlooker would take one glance at the couple and feel able to safely make the assumption they were two people who had a handle on the direction in which their lives were going. That fact that they did not was of no consequence. One thing that they did know, and were reminded of as soon as they entered this part of town, was that as long as they looked like they did then everything was alright.

They moved along the street, undeserved sensations of superiority blossoming within them as they glanced around at all the other people sat nearby. All these people who probably hadn't even come close to trying to do what they had just done. The next day crushing doubt would come. But for now they were immune.

At one point the free space on the pavement narrowed due to a set of chairs and tables spilling out of a cafe's allocated outdoor area. Occupied and thus unable to be moved by waiters fearing that in doing so they would be violating their customerisalwaysright protocol, these obstacles forced the man to pause so that his wife could move on through and squeeze between the wayward dining area and the parked cars on the curb.

During his momentary pause he looked around him and had his expectations fulfilled. She was there. Whoever she was. She must have followed them. They had walked down this way, so she must've gathered that there was a fair chance they would return by the same route. She was distracted now, though. She didn't even glance up. She was intently eating some sort of glorified sandwich with a flag stuck in the top bun. Like everybody around her, a notebook rested on the table next to whatever it was she had ordered. Unlike everybody else, she did not appear to be writing poetry.

<u>Chocofix – a cereal worthy of idolatry!</u>

"Did you see that they do breakfast in the court canteen?"

"…"

"There I was, preparing rushed breakfasts before I left the HQ and dashing out. I have to get a stupidly early bus as there's only one every two hours and getting the next one would make me late, you see. So I always had an hour of sitting around when I got here."

The 'HQ' Olwyn was talking about was actually her flat. This was one of her carefully concocted eccentricities. As you can no doubt see: very endearing.

"Now I just eat here. Extra twenty minutes in bed instead of making breakfast, and something to kill the time when I arrive. Perfect. I did it today."

"…"

"And you know what shocked me? They're still selling Chocofix. The breakfast cereal."

"…"

"I wondered if they would stop selling it while this case was on. Is it appropriate?"

"…"

"I guess he's innocent until proven guilty, and all that."

"…"

"Have you ever tried Chocofix?"

"…"

"They taste alright, but I always feel a bit funny about these foods that sort of advertise themselves using slogans that are meant to sound religious. Like that American barbecue place. Bible menus and all that. I feel weird about it."

"..."

"They are shaped like a cross. Not like noughts and crosses. Like a Jesus cross."

I knew.

"And that's why I'm not sure about them. But they taste good so I always have a crisis of conscience when I eat them."

"..."

"And given the circumstances, that crisis is even more intense at the moment..."

"..."

"Not that I'm religious really, I just worry I might be offending someone, somewhere."

I vaguely acknowledged this with a blink.

"Have you done any background reading for this guy?"

"..."

"I know we're not supposed to, but I wanted to look into him. Apparently he's very strange. Obviously he's rich. He owns Chocofix. But he spends all his time in an empty room watching TV or something. I read a profile on the internet."

I'd read the same profile.

"If that's true then I'm not surprised he makes his cereal into weird shapes."

A loud laugh from her. I failed to see the reason for it. The person on the other side of me started to drag at the roll of paper mounted on the wall that separated us.

"Anyway, I had some of them today, some Chocofix, and, you'll never guess, lucky me, I shook the cereal into the bowl – now don't ask me why they don't sell those little single-serving boxes, I don't know, but I agree with you that one big box might be unhygienic – and out came the toy!"

Another laugh. Sometimes people can find too much joy in the everyday.

"So I opened the packet – bright orange it was – and the series of toys they are doing now are like those binoculars things."

"…"

"But not binoculars. Like the eye bit looks like binoculars, but you don't see out of the other end. Instead you see a picture. I think normally the picture is supposed to rotate or change or something, but this was a freebie so it was just one image."

"…"

"You'll never guess what the picture was. It was dead strange."

"Go on."

"It was two people, bent over a desk, writing. On the desk was a book. Pretty boring, really."

Abolition

She stared at her phone screen on the bus. She had been asked to sign a petition. A black rap artist had been booked to headline a major festival and a group of people numbering exactly one-oh-seven-and-counting were outraged. They wanted a 'rock band'; deduce what you may. The 'I'm-not-racist-buts' were coming thick and fast. Now one-oh-eight. The slogan at the bottom of the page asked her to 'prevent this abolition'. She grimaced. Every time she looked at her phone things seemed to get uglier.

The bus stopped. It was time, if she had counted correctly. She had. As she suspected, they moved to get on. It had taken hanging around outside the chip shop and waiting for the night bus but she had learned where they got off at night. And after a bit of trial and error Jenny also learned that, much earlier in the morning than she usually got the bus, they caught it here. She had planned her new routine so she could plausibly establish herself as some sort of fellow local who shared a bus journey. They wouldn't bat an eyelid.

It had been boring; all that waiting around in the disused garage across the street from the chip shop until they locked up. They worked late hours it seemed, and they carried on writing in the fucking book even after the two a.m. closing time. The two-thirty night bus and she hadn't even been pissed. The sacrifices one makes for art and all that. Their home stop was about six closer to the chippy than hers was.

Their destination today was, as always, their place of work. Jenny planned to give it another stop after the couple got off and then double back and watch them go about their day jobs. She had spent the night beforehand trying to figure out how she could regularly make multiple visits to the chip shop in one day without either looking crazy, wasting a lot of good food or putting on an enormous amount of weight.

The woman was having difficulty removing herself from the red metal bar that passed for a bench in the bus shelter. The strap from her bag had looped itself around the end of the bar, and as she stood up quickly it pulled taut, preventing her from standing completely upright. It took her a while to catch up with Jenny in noticing what was impeding her movement. She tugged twice before craning her neck round her shoulder to see what was happening. The man was on the bus doorstep and he too turned, evidently sensing that she was not as close to him as usual. Jenny found it strange how couples sometimes managed that. She had never been able to do it. She could carry on walking for a good fifty metres before she realised she was alone. The man was waiting; his instinct had been correct and the woman was indeed lagging. No sign of impatience from the bus driver. The woman loosened her strap from the bench and skipped after the man, looking more harried than ever. The couple boarded the bus and sat down in the seats near the front that were perpendicular to the majority. They looked ahead and did not blink.

Comfortable in her knowledge that they would not get off for another seven stops, Jenny reverted her gaze to her phone. She started to keep count of the bus stops in her head, and by the time she had reached two she was engrossed by an article telling her about the things she ought to have learned in her twenties. She could barely remember herself then, but she still found herself feeling full of a regret that she knew, deep down, she didn't deserve to be feeling.

Having subconsciously tuned her ears to the faintly foreign accents of the couple she now sometimes (and secretly) referred to collectively as her muse, Jenny was distracted from her article-induced cocktail of pseudo-nostalgia and nostalgic guilt by the word 'look'. It was pronounced staccato and directed her voyeuristic gaze down the length of an outstretched arm and towards a pointing finger. She was up to number three in her head. Five stops to go, then she could stand up and disembark. The finger was pointing at a laminated poster, nailed to a telegraph pole. The pointer's companion made a sound indicating curiosity – an 'oooh' or an 'ahah' or something – and began to read what they could make out, unwittingly managing to do so in perfect synchronisation with Jenny. Sitting further down the bus than the other two were, Jenny had longer to see the poster before they passed it. Consequently she seemed to make out a greater number of the words. The couple, she noticed, were writing down what they had seen in another of their notebooks, and stopped after writing what Jenny guessed was about eight words. She assumed they would be the first eight: 'Song Street Books' Publishing Arm: Fiction, Academic, Poetry...'

Jenny had seen more, but felt she only needed to remember what they knew. She felt closer to them in this way. She felt she might be able to channel what they were feeling at this point if she restricted herself to knowing only what they knew.

The Bar that was a Toilet Once

The place was small. Too small for a gig really, but I liked the beer list and the sort of people in there so I snapped at the chance to finally play it. Thirty minutes, a couple of free pints, then another half hour. Background music really, nothing else. I was conscious that I had a really, really good jukebox to compete with and at any moment some prick could turn that on. Plus it had already been on, establishing itself. A tough act to follow.

A cuboid. A box. Essentially a smallish box – underground – with some grotty but artistic toilets at one end and a bar at the other. And it's brilliant.

It's seven-thirty and I'm conscious that I'm due on soon, so I'll outline to you what I perceive my surroundings to be like and then I'll get cracking.

Thanks to the flashing and blinking lights of the jukebox I can see a strip somewhere near the centre of the bar more clearly than I can see the rest; not even the bar is lit that well in here. Within this twinkling red-and-amber strip there is a table, the people sat at it ungratefully receive the glow of the flashing bulbs – they shield their eyes regularly as they lean in to make conversation over the volume of the music, which I would call appropriately loud. It gives the place an atmosphere; when I was trying to go through what I thought was a beat phase this is the sort of thing I imagined a dive bar to be like. You can, if you talk quite loudly, maintain a conversation.

You can think before you speak, too, in here. People all over the place are thinking before they start speaking. A prime spot for dates in my world. On one of my two dates I came here. You have to think before you speak a lot on dates if you are like me and, when under pressure to perform, often fall into the trap of trying to sound clever and ending up sounding vacuous. You'll get what I'm talking about in a bit; I have a song about fucking post-futurism. But anyway, in dates quasi-intellectualism is a bad move, as I have come to realise. I won't digress any further.

The two people sat at the table under the flashing jukebox lights with their hands over their eyes are leaning into each other to aid the audibility of their conversation. They are the only people I can see in any sort of detail through the murk – which I am exaggerating, I admit. I must put some of the lack of definition of my surroundings down to what I suspect is my failing eyesight and mediocre concentration span. They look like exactly the sort of people I'd expect to see down here. Smart. As in mentally. More so than I am. Perhaps even more so than Ralph who, unsurprisingly, has not shown up. The woman must be hot though, in that massive coat. I can't see their faces or anything but their demeanour gives me these impressions. Anyway, my point is that they are thinking for a long time before they speak. And not just a long enough time to sit back and have a sip of their respective pints. I mean

76

longer. Enough time to sit back, have a sip, look all clever and ponderous, then say what you have just cooked up in your massive academic brain.

I'm due on in five, the barman tells me. 'Due on' is a rich phrase. Technically I'm already 'on'. I'm sitting here, by the window that looks out onto the back stairs, on my stool. The only thing that'll change is that my pint will find its way to a spot where it is precariously balanced on the slip of a windowsill and my guitar will find its way onto my lap.

I'm on. We're on. Consider yourself invested. I suppose you have to be. You're here now. I'm sorry to tell you that I'm not playing any of the songs you might have heard from the album today. Just my solo stuff, under my new pseudonym. You won't know it.

I've decided to open with what I consider to be my most attention-grabbing song. By that I chiefly mean that it is the one that throws in a casual 'fuck' within the first verse. When I'm stripped down to just my guitar and myself (and I sometimes chuck in a harmonica, key of C, that I can sometimes play better that I can at other times) I have to rely on what I say to grab attention. Especially when the music is sometimes pretty mediocre. Even I admit that, to myself, when I'm assessing my life and feeling at my lowest. They probably think I reckon I'm Elliot Smith.

I hate the sound of my own voice. It's more obvious in small rooms like this. The speaker is practically behind my head – my own words being blasted back at me as soon as I have let them go. It's like a circuitous assault on my ego. Probably needed. Every now and again us artistic types need that sort of thing. The first – upon graduation – is hard to deal with. Before that it's all your friends telling you how impressive it is that you've written a novel by age twenty or that you can write songs. Apparently you're really talented, and you'd better believe it. Then, clutching an upper second-class degree in something like literature, you are cast out from that place, wherever it is. The necessity of the practical 'thing on the side'. You work in book shops and play to half-listening crowds. Or you write books and do hack work – if you can get it, and that comes after more expensive training – to support yourself. Or not even that, really. Just to keep your chin above the water. Your nose only submerging every few seconds or so, you bob desperately, putting on a brave face and acting as if you expected this and never secretly thought that you, just you, and for no particular reason other than that you are talented and impressive and had produced that stuff by age only twenty, would just stumble into something. That you would be one of those. You'd be spotted. Online. At a reading. At a gig. Amongst all the other no-hopers, you would stand out because you spent two years at a student radio station or had a few short stories published in a trendy periodical. Not likely. Much more realistic: You fester on the outskirts in a shit flat you chip-less-than-fair-share-to with a mate who works in computers and subs you. But remember, you're the arty one. Look at all that integrity. It suits you almost as much as that fitted suit does. Shame about the cuffs poking out there. Nice socks.

So, voice bouncing directly into the back of my head, I'm a few songs in. This is flying by. We're a good half of the way through now. Nobody's stood up yet, but I guess it's not that sort of place. The bloke from behind the bar brought me another pint, and I don't think he's going to bother charging me for it. This is living. One person is paying rapt attention. This woman near the front. And in this bar the woman being near the front means I keep accidentally kicking her knee as I bob my leg up and down, keeping time. Perhaps she is unable to avoid paying attention since I keep nudging her the way I do, but I'd like to think she was sat here at the front for a reason. Maybe she's a journalist. She has a notebook. Maybe she'll give me a write-up that nobody will ever care about. I could stick it up on my wall. With a drawing pin or something. Sorry, I'm going a bit off topic. It's because at the moment I'm playing an instrumental, and during this song I often tend to allow my mind to wander whilst muscle memory kicks in. It's one of the perks of not being productive enough a writer to have created a large back catalogue. I've played these songs countless times, so I barely need to think. I've only a couple of songs after this, and after that my attention will be fully devoted to the pragmatic and diligent documentation of this evening. Perhaps in a manner similar to that of the lady down at the front here. She's writing, however only when looking away – towards the jukebox. Maybe she's a health-and-safety person. An electrician or something. I do sometimes wonder how a machine with that many records inside it can stay mounted on the wall like that. Maybe she's a physicist.

And we're done. Clever that, how I managed to keep thinking about other things whilst I was playing, wasn't it? Or perhaps damning of my work ethic.

After the gig I pack my stuff away and make a conscious decision to mingle. Such a decision involves sitting at the bar for a bit and hoping that people who watched, or even partially watched, come up and say hello. To be honest I'm quite pissed off that Ralph, true to form, has failed to show up. I like to think I can bounce off another person and use them to meet new people. We can witter on about travelling holidays that we have fictionalised purely for the purpose of having something to talk about. People will be impressed, consider us worthy companions for the evening and then we can try to befriend them, just like Ralph claims he used to do with exotic and intelligent people during his month in Budapest that never happened. I know those stories are not real and I still feel jealous when I hear them.

Nobody comes over, and the barman's replies to my attempts at conversation are rapidly shortening. I am uncomfortably aware that I am that bloke at the bar who is a little drunk and mistakenly believes his anecdotes are interesting as opposed to annoying. And I get hideously self-aware after a few. So I make the relatively terrifying decision to go and see if that woman I kept nudging is still there. Failing that, I'll stand by the jukebox in the hope that the intellectual-looking couple ask me what I'm putting on and then I'll say something like PIL and they'll condone my decision and that will be the beginning of a fruitful, artistic, intelligent and totally-fulfilling-to-the-point-that-I-forget-that-I-need-other-friends-as well sort of relationship. Like with fucking Ralph early on. My mistake. I'm now sure that he genuinely doesn't need friends.

<u>Surfaces</u>

Jenny's legs were slightly too long for their allocated space under the table she shared with the even-taller lady, who had entered the bar about twenty minutes ago and unapologetically blocked her view of the jukebox and those near it. All that the tall woman had said to her so far had concerned the performance that had ended just as she had entered. The tall lady had done a poor job of feigning dismay when told that this performance had come to a halt before she had even heard one song. She appeared to want to seem worried that she might have offended somebody. Then they didn't speak for a while.

Before long this sitting and occasionally excusing the clashing of legs was not satisfactory. Middle-aged: yes. But beyond fun on an evening out, in a relatively respectable establishment: no.

Jenny attempted to have a conversation, every so often trying to subtly crane her neck past the extravagant bouffant that sat atop the tall lady's head and get a glimpse at the people she had followed here. The tall lady opened her heavily lipsticked mouth in reply, plucking a small paper flag from behind her ear before she spoke.

"Ha! Underground. Quite literally. You know, I bet everybody says what you just said. And what I just said."

The lips closed again with an almost-squelch and seemed to be stuck fast – the excessive application of makeup working to fulfil Jenny's silent demands. She felt a little offended. Her sense of her own originality wounded. But at least the lips were now closed. But wait: they opened again.

"You know that some of the people here probably work for ITV or something."

Jenny saw no relevance in this comment so did not reply.

"Another place that would satisfy you. I know another place that would satisfy you."

She looked a little smug. Salesman-like. Jenny desperately wanted to think of something caustic to say.

"Found myself in a book shop the other day. Nice little place. Really hard to find. You get the impression that only those who really look ever find it."

"..."

"You know what I think about places like that?"

"Go on." Jenny took a sip of her pint and watched it reduce – the lipstick smirk was still visible through the warped lens of the base of the glass.

"That." Lipstick paused here. "Is subculture."

Another pause for Jenny's response. Jenny tried to hold her stare but started to feel uncomfortable.

She said: "I'll check it out. I like things like that. Cheers."

The tall lady took a slug from her drink.

"No, you don't understand. I stress the 'is'. That shop is subculture. This isn't. That over there isn't. The bookshop I am speaking of is. It's the only example left. Subculture exists within its walls. It's beautiful."

"Okay."

"And reasonably priced..."

At this point the man who had been playing the music wandered over. He mumbled an excuse to join and made surprised eye contact with the tall lady. His legs added to the uncomfortable tangle beneath the table as recognition between the two of them became obvious but was not mentioned.

"Nice to see you." This was said by the musician to the tall lady. It was not said pleasantly. Jenny noticed the use of 'see' and not 'meet' and asked no questions. She looked away from the table and saw the people she actually wanted to speak to get up and leave the emptying bar. Jenny decided she'd better be making her excuses before things got even worse.

Slim

"Cut that out."

He was reading a paragraph aloud and drumming his fingers on the kitchen table. The redraft. She was instructing. Soon it would be time to swap. This is how they did things. Imperative balance. The redraft.

She was sipping from a slightly dented can of ale – her swallows punctuating her instructions. It took him a long time to begin to wonder where she was finding the time to breathe in this arrangement.

He did what he was told. It was nearly finished. Formatted according to the extraordinarily specific guidelines listed on the publishing firm's otherwise completely unhelpful website. There had not even been an address on there. It seemed that one had to use the information on the internet, along with the information on the poster, as well as a significant amount of assumption in order to have any success with these people.

They swapped positions.

She was poised over the printouts, looking expectantly at her partner.

"What next?"

The man pointed out that he hadn't actually finished carrying out the final instruction. They went back to their previous positions and he did just that. Then they swapped back again. The woman took initiative this time and began reading, pausing only once over the next five minutes to point out a grey hair in the man's stubble that she had noticed three days ago.

To the left of her left hand was the black notebook. The one that had come to dominate their lives over the past few months. Full of names and details. Chip fat stained many of the pages and had caused some of the ink to smudge. In places they'd had to use their own judgement to discern the names of some of the clients, deciphering the meaning of the smudges based on parts of the names that they could see uninhibited.

The man instructed the rewriting of a sentence he had rewritten a few minutes ago. Thus was the nature of this activity. And it might still be poor. They had to try to prepare themselves for disappointment. They had not tried anything like this before, so they were not sure how it would go.

The phone rang. This was expected and they looked at the clock. Exactly the right time.

"That'll be the benefactor." That was what they called him now, half jokingly.

The man walked over to the phone and answered. It was nothing out of the ordinary. The usual check up. Is everything going according to plan? Are you happy with it? GIMME BACK ALL MY MONEY. Ahah, only joking, you know I back you all the way, I wouldn't have invested otherwise! Glad it's working out. This could be our big thing, you know. All this followed by an abrupt goodbye.

The man looked at the cracked plaster on the ceiling.

"Thank fuck for him."

The woman looked up and asked him if everything was alright. The man told her that it was; that it had just been the usual phone call. They were set to go whenever they wanted.

"You know, I still feel uneasy relying on rich folk to enable us to do what we do."

"He turned up just when we needed him. We had no other option."

"I know."

"He's punctual. At least."

"At least."

"And we eat for free. Even when we get sick of chips, we still get to eat for free."

"Out of bowls..."

"But free."

"With, or without, milk."

"But free."

"Condiments optional."

It was about three o'clock. They had been at it four hours, maybe five. It hadn't felt like work; it had felt like a race. Driven by an eagerness to have a finished product: a slim stack of paper, double sided to save whatever made them feel most righteous. Ink. Paper. Time. It didn't matter, really. They were beyond trying to find reasons to like the people that they were. They were focused on what was on the page and what needed to be done to keep it there.

"Let's take a break."

It was still sunny outside, on the cracked cement that bordered the patchy lawn. Victorian grandeur gone stale surrounded them. All of their neighbours were exactly alike in the sense that they were totally unique. Not even purposefully. No artistes here, just strugglers.

The man and the woman thought about what they were doing. All they had to do was go back to work and they could be free in one sense, albeit at the cost of another. They'd bend over backwards to intensify their situation, though. As long as it could one day take paperback form.

The woman lit a cigarette – expensive tobacco imported from somewhere in Spain. Or, at least, that was what the Danish guy who introduced and sold it to her had said. It had a figure in a headdress on the front. She breathed out smoke into the man's face and he turned his face away. He didn't mind that much, though. He walked over to the fence and took a furtive glance over it, then bent down to look through a hole in a panel midway up. Nothing on the other side, he ascertained, and moved back towards the woman. He told her this and her shoulders relaxed a little and she started to inhale more smoothly on her cigarette. They both knew why they had come out here.

They could hear the football fans in the distance. The sound of people made them both hungry for human contact and the woman stubbed out her cigarette and took the man by the hand. The man picked a lump of food from the furthest back of his molars and looked at the woman. They went inside.

Dire Tribe

It was a week after that gig I was telling you about. It had been a dull one so I skimmed through most of it. Just made sure I ate, slept, shat etc. Fulfilled my basic requirements to continue to qualify as a living animal.

I was in Bill's house. The football was on the television.

For some reason when I was younger I always thought that music and football were completely separate. Incompatible. I didn't think that people like Bill – whose radio show I had been a fan of for a number of years; whose taste in music meant that I considered him to be a kind of benchmark for cool and taste – would pass their time watching something as primitive as football seemed to be to me.

I enjoyed the game actually. And I must admit, I don't mind putting my minimal (I like to think minimalist) skills to the test with a bit of a kickabout every now and again. My issue is with football as an institution, because it makes so many people think they are being clever when they aren't. It gives so many middle-aged know-it-alls a platform to criticise trained professionals as if they could do a better job themselves. The same middle-aged know-it-alls who snap almost immediately whenever somebody else dares to question their proficiency at whatever day job it is they hold down.

"Trust me Gary. I've been doing this job twenty years. What you need (...) no (...) I'm telling you, what you need is to take it apart, give it a good oiling, and it'll be good as new. (...) Well you've not done it right then. I've been (...) no (...) I've been doing this for twenty years, I think I know. Do it agai-*FU*cking hell did you see that. Bloody useless that lad (...) me too, we were both right. Called it from the start. Eleven million for that sack of shit (...) too right. Me too. I could've signed a better player from down the park."

Fucking go and do it then.

Bill's of that school and I find it disappointing. He knows people who have nothing in common with him other than a shared support of a football team. But that's enough for them to form an alliance. Unified, defending one another regardless of the argument. Eyes never leave the screen at times like these. If you'll forgive the vulgarity: I could've got away with a wank in that room during the game. It made conversation difficult.

"At that gig I did the other week..."

"GO ON..."

"At that gig I did the other week..."

"GO ON..."

"At that gig I did the other week..."

"Sorry Ezra, wasn't listening just then, go on."

"There was this woman who seemed to be taking notes. I was pretty drunk, so I didn't pay much attention really, but this stuck in my head."

"What were they notes of? Did you get a glance?"

"I.."

"GO ON..."

"I..."

"Sorry, go on."

"I eventually went to have a chat with her but she left pretty quickly. I did sneak a glance though when she was staring past my head at something."

"Hmmm?"

"I did manage to get a glance."

"What did it say? Must be interesting if you're telling me."

"It was just lists of, like, body language or something. What I saw was anyway."

"What sort of body language?"

Only one eye was on the football now.

"Points at drink they want with left hand. Stride-like gait. Half-smiles whenever he finishes a long sentence. Raises eyebrow when asking a question. Looks to nearest exit often. Things like that. They were what I saw."

"You memorised it all?"

"Yeah."

"Think they were about you? You were on stage, right. So you'd be centre of attention. Maybe she kept on watching afterwards."

"Hmmm."

"Reviewer?"

"Don't think..."

"Hang on till half-time and I'll do a test."

Fifteen minutes later, during half-time, Bill made me walk up to the dresser and pretend to order a drink. He stood on the other side of it holding two bottles: one real ale, one Coke. He said he was deaf so I'd have to point to what I wanted and then he whispered for me to do so without thinking about it too much. I tried. I pointed with my right hand. Afterwards, Bill pointed out that I had not raised my eyebrow when I asked him which hand I had pointed with.

So it wasn't me. I was a little disappointed. I think I had been subconsciously hoping that she fancied me or something ridiculous like that. Weird.

The atmosphere deteriorated quite rapidly after that. Whatever group of beshorted adults Bill was rooting for started to lose – or at least seemed to; the score was still nil-nil – and Bill's words became exclusively directed towards the TV. I supposed he must be used to talking to inanimate things. Microphones, televisions. Never sure if there was anybody on the other end. Never sure if anybody cared what he had to say. He did work on local radio, after all.

I resigned myself to an afternoon spent sunken into the settee alongside Bill, being informed every now and again of the opinions of somebody neither of us really knew. A person who relied upon the medium of one hundred and forty characters, or however much it was now, in order to convey their undying, sports-related wit.

Another gripe of mine: football humour. It works like currency. Traded with and regurgitated by other members of the group in return for short-lived respect and momentary status as the person in the group who was well and truly in the know that day. An immediate swap for temporary but desperately needed authority. A revitalising shock to an ego floundering. That keeps you going, above water. One more life gained as a safety net in case you should commit the worst crime of them all: offer up the misinformed piece of trivia. That is enough to validate a good ten-minute-long ostracising. You're fucked then, until somebody is kind enough to correct you and make up some reason as to why you might have been right at one point, but were just a little out of date with your proclamation. It's easy to get confused. Then it's your round, and you're back in.

I like it, though. Sort of. If something crops up where some sort of nugget of knowledge I happen to have picked up at some point can be appropriately injected for smartarse points then I jump at the opportunity. Perhaps I'm a hypocrite. Perhaps I'm bitter.

As the match was drawing to an end Bill's brother Angus – my flatmate – popped over for a chin wag and brought us on to the topic of an advert that was doing the rounds on TV. I really must tell you about this.

Smile past the camera, walnut-infused, sleeping beyond what's needed

Jenny was following the couple from the chip shop again. She didn't think they had noticed her yet. She'd only been to the chippy twice a week for the past five weeks – nothing too unusual really. And just short of half of those times it had been operating on that bizarre self-service system. Jenny had dutifully written in the book each time, taking the liberty of having a snoop around the previously filled-in pages in return for her efforts. The question she was asked usually changed on a weekly basis, sometimes more often. She had told them what newspaper she read, about her most recent memory that had nothing to do with herself, the names of her great-grandparents, her favourite colour from amongst the top five of those that she considered the most unattractive. All of this alongside whatever it was she bought and in what quantity. Sometimes she was asked to wait in the shop whilst she was eating, if possible, and provide one answer before she ate and another afterwards. It was all very strange.

She was following them through a posh area of town. Jenny did not know the name of the area but recognised it from travelling through frequently. It was early evening; sunny; warmish. The couple looked to be going on an ordinary evening stroll. Jenny's estimate, based on memories of mostly ignored bus journeys, was that they were about halfway between the bus stop near their house and the city centre. That night, though, they had opted to walk the whole way in. A reasonably lengthy walk, but not an unpleasant one.

Jenny was doing her best to ensure that a few people were always between herself and the couple. Although comfortable that she had not yet been identified as a follower, she was well aware that the more often they saw her, the closer they might come to establishing such an opinion. She needed to be at most vaguely recognisable to them. She must not become a regular feature in their consciousness until she was sure she wanted to. She knew that she would have to talk to them at some point. She didn't know what she would say. She didn't suppose it was common for somebody to pick a person at random and decide to use them and their lives as inspiration for their breakout creative endeavour. She supposed this behaviour was especially odd when its subject was a couple of chip shop owners, however intellectual and quirky they appeared to be. In short, Jenny was well aware that what she was doing was very strange and probably getting close to illegal. She reassured herself that this was often the case with revolutionary artistic activity, and settled within that rut of justification for the time being. That way, she could also convince herself that whatever it was she was doing might yield fruit that was both artistic and noteworthy. Something to make her feel she had contributed something, in some way.

Jenny had taken to carrying a notebook, in which she had been attempting to document all that she saw on her travels. This had proven completely unhelpful so far, and would certainly seem highly suspicious if anybody else found it and read what was inside. The recording of mundane details always attracted unwanted attention, Jenny thought. She had already used up about half of the notebook, and she was starting to wish she had written in pencil. The dwindling amount of space was making her worry that she would fill up her first notebook dedicated to this new section of her life with rubbish. Counterproductively, this was driving her to take more and more notes so as to make sure that she did not neglect to write down something that might, with hindsight, turn out to be something she wished she had taken down precisely. So she was now writing as she walked, sidestepping bollards and feeling conflicted about the fact that while she was at least doing something, which felt good, it could prove to have more of a negative end result than doing nothing would have. This feeling was familiar.

Nevertheless, positivity was there, as she scribbled and power walked after the couple, who were increasing their speed. Jenny was buoyed in the way that hobbyists are buoyed by the pleasure they get in the sheer volume of their collections. The process of amassing is pleasurable in itself to some. In spite of her worries Jenny was quickly finding herself pleased by this process. She was building a collection of information concerning the day-to-day lives of these people. Even if much of it was mundane, it was still useful for character profiling. She was getting a genuine feeling for how they behaved when they were comfortable that they were not under scrutiny. She was starting to feel like she knew them, but not enough so that any major revelation would shock her. Jenny had been thinking about this. If you knew somebody well, then the acquisition of a significant piece of new information about them can be unsettling. Something like finding out that your dad used to be a porn actor or you gran once held up a corner shop. Those sorts of things enforce a radical re-evaluation of the character you once thought you knew inside out. However, learning information about people you do not know intimately is interesting. It is why people trawl through gossip magazines or sit up and read Wikipedia pages about musicians at night-time. You form a sort of distant opinion – a fluid preconception that you can work with, but do not feel compelled to ditch, or even worse, feel betrayed by, should you ever come across something that seriously contradicts your perception of the person. Jenny wanted to build her relationship with these people, but at a safe distance. She was happy to amass information for the time being. The more she gathered this way, the less – if any at all – would have to be gleaned from any direct contact.

As Jenny found herself spending more of her

time absorbed in what she was now calling her work, she was feeling an increasingly steep decline in her desire to interact with any of her friends or colleagues. Everything else was becoming a hindrance.

Jenny looked up from a particularly long note she had been making about the frequency at which the man wore the particular scarf he had chosen to wear that day and found herself in a square. She grimaced and looked around her, irritated. She pocketed her pen and notebook. The couple were nowhere to be seen.

The square was alive with activity. At each corner was a spotlight. These illuminated the space occupied by a tall office block undergoing building work, which stood at one end of the square. A crane with a sort of basket on the end – the kind found on a cherry picker – stood in the centre of the square. Jenny looked down and saw that she had a red-and-white striped ribbon semi-stuck to her waist, the ends trailing around her ankles. At closer inspection, She could see a number of cameras. She looked for a sound boom and saw none.

A fat man came hurrying through the half light towards her. She stopped walking and waited for him. Upon arrival he gestured towards her and looked irritated. He berated her tardiness and asked why she had chosen those particular clothes. He then decided that it didn't matter, and steered her towards the office block. For some reason Jenny did not resist.

Once inside the building Jenny stood in darkness until a man shone a torch into her face and made noises of approval. The lights in the building – if there were any – were never turned on. Jenny was led through the dark room by the man with a torch and was directed up some stairs, the handrail of which was decorated with glowing stickers to guide the way. She ascended, not really knowing why, and was aware of footsteps following her up, accompanied by the panting of a person who sounded unfit enough to be the fat man she had met first. He was, she guessed, a couple of landings below her with the gap increasing due to the disparity between their physical conditions.

After a while the man released a distressed yelp that sounded something like 'stop' and she did. About a minute later his soggy bulk bumped into her from behind and he apologised. He then shone his torch ahead of them and Jenny saw that they were in front of a door marked as an exit. She had no idea how the man had managed to judge the point at which she would reach this door. The man knocked three times and shouted through to somebody called Ralph, who opened the door a crack and passed through a piece of thick black cloth. The fat man then used his sweaty hands to tie this around Jenny's head and then opened the door. Still, Jenny did not ask what was going on. Instead she patted her pocket to check that her notebook was safe, and started attempting to commit all of what was going on to memory. She felt certain that she could work this into her project in some way.

When the door opened she felt cold air on her partially shrouded face. The fat man gently pushed her forwards and she started to walk, guided by a significantly slimmer hand that she assumed belonged to Ralph. She was shivering now that the sun had set, despite the heat of what she knew to be industry-standard stage lighting. They walked and, just as Jenny felt her toes reach a point at which they were no longer supported by anything, stopped. A strange serenity had passed over her. Ralph let go of her hands and stepped back. He told her to be careful not to overbalance. He told her that there was no bungee or anything, as that would make it less realistic. He told her all she had to do was what she was told, for just thirty seconds or so, and then she could step back and everything would be fine. Then he told her to spread her arms out like she was being crucified.

Jenny followed all these strange instructions, curling her toes around the edge of the building.

She started to count to thirty.

Two skinny hands shoved her back and she stumbled forwards.

Her mouth snapped open in a gasp so violent that her jaw felt out of place.

She fell in an upright position, like she was doing a pencil jump at the swimming pool.

She landed, still perfectly upright, with a

clanging sound. The floor bounced beneath her.

There was a popping sound and Jenny was showered with light, solid, small objects.

She stepped forward again, searching for somewhere to rest her hands and breathe deeply.

As she did this, one of the light, small, solid objects crunched underneath her foot.

Ralph told her to remove the blindfold and Jenny found herself on the cherry picker platform. She had fallen about three feet. Ralph was grinning at her. He told her that they'd pay her more than she was expecting. Cash, too. They'd had to do it that way because they needed the look of horror on her face. And wow, they had it. Shock sells, he told her. This was a shocker.

Jenny thought that was just about it for her, as far as she was concerned, in the world of acting. She once got told that you just stumble into the most amazing things that happen in your life. This felt like a mixed bag.

The crane lowered her down to the ground, where she was greeted by the fat man. He thanked her, said they'd be in contact again if they needed more work, and told her to watch out for herself on television. She was given four hundred pounds cash.

Decor

"I like to think of myself as somebody who does not just wear clothes, but somebody who decorates their body with clothes in order to make a point."

"..."

I could not see her clothes, for obvious reasons. However I remembered, from the jury room, that she had been wearing something very similar to what I was wearing. I considered myself somebody who wore clothes, and sought not to decorate themself with them.

"It's important, I think. It goes with my role in society, if you follow. Need to be respectable, you know."

"..."

"Give off a good impression. Nobody wants to be checked out by somebody who looks a shambles."

Bafflingly, Olwyn had turned out to be – or at least claimed to be – a doctor of some sort. A medical one.

"..."

"Nothing too fancy. I like it to be businesslike but friendly. Still professional though. I'm not there to chat."

"..."

"You don't seem to follow. I'll elaborate anecdotally for the sake of clarity. If you don't mind."

Fucking brilliant.

"The other week I was sent this guy who'd been

suffering for a long time with obstructive sleep apnoea."

"I imagine that's common."

"Hmmm, I assume. Anyway, he was sent in and I was wearing my usual sort of outfit – affably businesslike, as I said. I looked at him and prescribed some things, gave a bit of advice, you know. The usual."

"..."

"Nothing out of the ordinary."

"..."

"Anyway, the bloke, after I'd given him all of the advice I thought he needed, still hung about. He gave me a once over and, to be honest, I think he liked what he saw."

Presumably they had never met before.

"Started telling me about how, a while ago, he worked in television. He told me this anecdote about a time when he was setting up for something and the actor was taking ages getting changed or something. He was waiting and a couple came up to him and pointed to a scissor lift or something that they were using and asked if it was high enough to kill you if you jumped off it."

"..."

"Anyway, he started to go on, about to start to go into detail about how it depended on some specific factor, before I cut him off."

"..."

"You see, that's why I wear the clothes. I don't

want to look like I'm there for a chat. I'm there to help, yes, but in a working context."

I opted out of highlighting how evident it was that the clothes scheme was not working.

"I took Hippocrates' Oath, you see. You know, that thing that all doctors have to say."

"It's pronounced Hip-ock-rat-ees. You say Hippocratic."

"Yeah, well whatever. I took that, and I continue to take it very seriously."

"Go on." I was now interested and wearing and wry grin. Olwyn was predictable.

"That stuff about not divulging a secret. Well I apply that to everything unrelated to medicine in my office. If it isn't about medicine I don't want to know."

Brilliant.

"There's a time and a place for incessant chit-chat. I don't need his opinions or stories or whatever."

"Too right. You don't."

"Now you get it."

"..."

"I decorate myself with clothes that create around me the environment in which I want to exist."

Regarding

Ralph often says he doesn't have a television, but he does. He keeps it in what is supposed to be a downstairs toilet – most likely for staff working in the shop – but actually functions as a storage cupboard. Sat on the toilet is a mannequin with a printout of Bill's clammy, white face glued to the front of its head, as if it was actually Bill.

When Ralph walked into Bill's living room he commented on how it was highly unusual for him to be in a room watching television, as he did not own one. Bill asked him how toilet Bill was and Ralph said he was in fine shape, apart from his left cheek, which was peeling away a little. Angus told him that he'd better get some glue and address that issue and Ralph agreed. Silence ensued, as everybody quickly realised that they had no news.

With a gesture like a limp handshake Angus guided attention back towards the television and hit play. Ralph pretended he did not know that you could pause live TV now and nobody commented. It was adverts. They were half way through, as they had been when Ralph walked in, so Angus started to rewind. After a few seconds Angus had ventured back to the midway point of the yoghurt advert that had run before the one he intended to rewatch. He pressed one more button to let it run and then set the remote control down on the arm of the chair he was sitting in.

A woman lay upon some sort of futon. Somebody who was supposed to sound French or something was murmuring about velvet and the woman on the screen was slowly inserting the spoon into her mouth. Her lips closed, and the spoon slithered out of her mouth, now sparkling clean, and was reinserted, assumedly in the hope that some remnant of the creamy substance was still on it. The French-sounding person made a low groaning sound and then a man with a full-on erection walked to centre screen and whispered at the viewer something about velvet again. Then a logo came on screen, the text dripping with white, creamy yoghurt. We were then told that this sort of yoghurt was available at all good supermarkets. I wondered if they had a version without bits for fussy children. Or if there were any bits at all. And then that advert was over.

Angus did another limp handshake gesture and paused the television. He checked that everybody was looking intently and pressed play. Within seconds Ralph informed everybody that he'd already seen this one; presumably on somebody else's television. The camera was panning towards a woman standing atop an office block of some sort.

The woman was blindfolded. Her toes curled over the edge of the building, but she did not look as if she were preparing to jump. Rather, upon close inspection, she was tilted carefully, slightly backwards, wary of the drop before her. I leaned nearer to the television and looked closely. The woman in the advert appeared to be counting under her breath. It was the woman from the bar. Now, you see, this is where I started to get a little worried. She was everywhere, it seemed. At least, she was everywhere I paid attention to my surroundings: in my subterranean local and on the television. Okay, only two, maybe three if I think a bit harder. But enough for a foundation layer of what I would call paranoia. She was still counting and I had been counting with her. She was up to twenty-two. Reasonably long advert. Must've cost a lot. At what I counted as twenty-five Ralph piped up.

"Now."

I didn't register at the time. I was enthralled. By this point the camera was zoomed in so that the woman's figure filled the television. Her feet were touching the bottom edge of the screen. She fell. The camera quickly zoomed in on her panicked face as it slid down the screen vertically. She wore a look of sheer horror, obvious even without seeing her eyes. The camera zoomed back out again as she landed in a metal, open topped cage attached to a long, thick, metallic arm. Small, brown rabbit-droppings-or-something showered the screen, and then it all went black. A logo filled the screen.

C H O C O F † X

It was spaced out like that: in capitals, with a gap between each letter. In keeping with the style used by lots of bands round these parts these days. Appealing to a certain demographic, perhaps.

"I recognised that woman."

"Aye, she was a bit of alright that one. Even with the blindfold."

"Fuck off, Angus."

"What do you mean then?"

"I mean that I recognised her."

"That's it?"

"That's it."

Angus sulkily turned his masturbatory glance elsewhere. After a few minutes of quiet he wandered off to no doubt rhythmically admire some of Bill's stash upstairs and return, all exercised out, to a displeased audience half an hour later. Bill paused the telly, which had been on since the advert, and left the room muttering about seeing if he could root out a few beers he thought he still had in the garage. He didn't have a garage.

Ralph turned to me and spoke for the first time since the advert.

"Where did you recognise her from?"

"My gig. And your shop, too."

"The gig in the toilet bar?"

"Yes, and also the shop. Just realised. She was wearing that jacket in the shop."

"Was it a good jacket?"

"Yes, that's why I recognised it."

"She was in the shop?"

"Yes. She bought some blank notebooks. And

some book about this French bloke. Or by a French bloke, or something like that. It was on The Shelf so I got extra cash from it, as per the rule."

"…"

"You were in the back at the time."

"Notebooks?"

"Yes."

"Black ones. Mole-something?"

"…"

"Good book, good jacket. Unfortunately buys branded notebooks, but I won't hold that against her as I was the one selling her them. Probably a good person. What was her name/phone number/ address?"

He grinned. That annoyed me.

"She just nearly fell off a building on TV."

"It was an advert."

"Yes."

"…"

"I think she's following me."

"Hmmm."

How to follow that

"Sadaka, you don't surf."

"Your point?"

"We're in Fallowfield."

"Again, your point?"

"..."

"Huh...?"

"Why the wetsuit?"

"It's not a wetsuit. It's practical urban camouflage, for nightcrawling."

"And why would you need that?"

"For my project."

"It highlights your tummy bulge."

"Fuck off."

"What project?"

"Secret."

Door slammed and the inquisitor was left in the narrow hallway. Sad had no time for the inquisitor. He had the whole night ahead of him. He seldom slept at nighttime.

Uber, minutes later. It had arrived so fast it made Sad wonder if it was possible that the driver had been round the corner waiting for him.

The centre of town was coldish.

Sad had not given the inquisitor a time he expected to be home. He'd never done that when they lived in the countryside, so he didn't see why he needed to all of a sudden. He rummaged in his backpack and pulled out his pride and joy and checked the zoom, removed the lens cap, night-vision mode on. Things went greenish.

The people in Manchester's Northern Quarter thought they were miracle workers sometimes. They thought they were exciting and new. But they sat in coffee shops and talked as if it was still thirty years ago. Home counties. Bucket hats. That equation.

Sad realised he was wearing one navy sock and one black one. Fuck. In the dark he'd at least struggle to notice this. The negative of an all-dark wardrobe was that you came to trust its obsidian nature blindly, to the point where it would fool you on an occasion such as this.

He sat on a doorstep and was told to move along by the homeless man whose knees he had just accidentally burdened with his bony, neoprene-clad arse. He moved along to the next doorstep, checked that it was vacant by pointing his night vision camcorder towards it, and sat down. He had been spending his evenings like this for a while now. He liked to watch people, see what they were up to, see if anything interesting happened.

Despite his efforts, Sad hadn't seen any genuine miracles. But he'd managed to capture – almost by accident – a comprehensive videographic cross section of hip-and-not-so Manchester from the vantage point of various doorsteps. And he'd only been vomited on twice, both times by men on stag dos looking for somewhere that did cheap Jagerbombs. He had watched – scraping sick from his clothing – five bald heads – bobbing and swaying above their ill-fitting blazers, bootcut jeans and dress shoes – recede into the semi-darkness. He had gone home early that night.

Just after seven p.m. was a good time for working on his project, Sad had learned. That time, before things got lewd, but after things had loosened. And in a greater sense, a time when things had yet to deteriorate into a non-place. A place stripped of its beauty by people capitalising on its perceived difference and thus making it the same as everywhere else. That was no doubt imminent. It had already started. But a few things still felt permanent.

Sad didn't even really know what constituted a miracle in his eyes. He didn't know if he was looking for something supernatural, or simply something that confirmed that things of note did actually happen. Perhaps that was miraculous enough. He had realised, from moving gradually urbanwards throughout his life, that the bigger your surroundings, the bigger something had to be for it to really count in any way. What he did know, though, was that whatever it is that he was looking for resided unequivocally within the potential of the human. And so he supposed he was effectively a people watcher; perhaps a people recorder.

The man whose knee he had recently sat upon was playing music – a reedy tune on a cheap instrument – in the hope that he may prize loose change from the consciences of people passing by.

A taxi stopped, doors opening as percussion for the reedy tune, and two people got out. Middle-aged, a little tweedy, bespectacled. One of them looked a bit like Sad's dad. A couple, perhaps. The man paid the taxi driver with a handful of change, mostly silvers. The taxi driver looked questioningly and shoved the change into his bumbag. The woman touched the man's arm and they threw some more silvers at the musician in the doorstep. They then did likewise to Sad, assumedly thinking his camera holding was some sort of avant-garde busking. Perhaps he was an arts student or something. He pocketed the change and watched as the couple consulted a road atlas with pencil markings all over it and made reference to shortcuts, betraying local knowledge which made Sad wonder why they needed the map. The man nodded towards the way they had come and mentioned a big brush. The woman seemed to agree, consenting silently, and they began to move in the indicated direction.

Another taxi pulled up and a gaudy woman stepped out, wobbling on her heels. She thanked the driver without paying and the driver pulled away without complaint. The woman turned to Sad and looked squarely at him. Her pale face filled the screen on his camcorder, tinted green. Her hair looked synthetic. She started to speak, scratching at a small scab on the left side of her chin as she did so.

"I'm looking for two friends who came by here."

Deep voice, laconic, educated.

"A couple?"

"I know nothing of their relationship."

"Man and woman?"

"Yes."

"By the big brush."

Sad had no idea that the people this unusual character was looking for were the couple he had just seen, but he felt that the three of them ought to meet in some way or another. He wanted to establish a connection between two sets of characters that was potentially completely unnecessary. An artistic form of human contact – if such a thing could ever exist.

The gaudy woman tottered off, keeping close to the wall at the side of the street and thus remaining shadowed. Sad zoomed in after her. Stuck in her beehive, just behind her left ear was a small paper flag on a cocktail stick – the kind you find stuck in gourmet-burgers to hold everything together. Sad got up and decided to follow.

The couple were stood opposite a huge statue of a brush that occupied a small garden area just off the street. They had a notebook out and were talking. The man prodded the statue with his brogue. The gaudy woman sat across the street, on the doorstep of a small art shop, watching them. Sad walked over to her and sat down on the doorstep next to her. She did nothing to stop him.

"You found them."

She did not answer. Sad looked at the woman and noticed how far her legs stretched out in front of her as she sat down. She scratched at the wound on her chin – which had now started bleeding – and looked briefly at him. She stuck out her hand.

"Theresa. Theresa Stern."

"Sad."

"Most of the time."

They shook and returned to staring. The woman took the little flag out of her hair and chewed the cocktail stick that served as the flagpole. She picked her teeth a little. She opened a can of lager that she had taken from her bag and drank it quickly. She pulled out a small notebook and wrote down a single, illegible sentence. At one point the couple at the big brush turned and seemed to look at them both directly. Sad wondered if they were shadowy enough in their doorstep to be unseen. Sad and Theresa stared back. Theresa wrote down another sentence. On the knuckles of her left hand – her writing hand – she had written, in green biro, the letters O, F, I and X. The I was stylised and the F was smudged.

Clea(n/r)ing

Grass was poking through the cracks in the bleached paving stones that covered the ground of the small, greasy-smelling space that they called 'out back'. They simultaneously wiped hands on their aprons and squinted skywards. They were hungry, but the idea of consuming what they sold – regardless of its irrefutable quality and standard of ingredients – was loathsome to them that day. Too much of a good thing.

They had made plans to try and start to wind things up. They didn't want the business to disappear suddenly, provoking questions.

The man bent down and pulled a tuft of grass from between his feet and threw it, watching it catch on a slight breeze and be lifted up, over the back fence, towards the place where they put the bins out. It had been a tiring, eventful past few weeks. The woman began to consider cleanliness.

They would often argue about the definition of clutter: whether or not such a term could be expanded to reference people; living things; bodies conscious of their own existence.

The questioning of such a matter had originated during a holiday they had embarked upon in the late nineties, where they had, for three nights only, stayed in a small encampment of two-man tents pitched on a beach in the south-west of Scotland. The sea had been perpetually still. The man in the next tent along had modelled himself on a film character renowned for his slacker outlook and penchant for drinking White Russians at any time of day. They had deduced that he did this because he hoped it helped to validate his potential alcoholism and his desire to inhabit a dressing gown as much as possible. Underneath that dressing gown he had worn a T-shirt upon which was emblazoned the slogan 'Your Future, Our Clutter', capitalised just like that.

The man had commented on how, as academics, the T-shirt was particularly relevant to them. He had argued that, due to the fact that they were becoming increasingly specialised and therefore increasingly useless via the acquisition of master's degrees and their ongoing PhDs, their future was inevitably bound to essentially irrelevant dialogue understandable to only a few, boring, over-read people living in fire hazards and chewing over things for far too long, only reaching a conclusion once everybody else had stopped caring what it was. He was the sort of guy that spoke in very long sentences. He told them that anybody who knew what it was that they were doing with themselves would consider them ineffectual and ultimately useless. But they would still consume; still breathe; still take up seating in busy places. And what was that? Useless but tangible? Clutter. And that necessitated some sort of cleanup.

As a result of this conversation, the man who would later go on to own a chip shop learned to worship the art of decluttering. If there was the possibility of making a pilgrimage to a geographical location that epitomised this modern desire to declutter, that would no doubt be where they would end up, sooner or later. She wondered if such a place existed. She wondered if such a place, by its very sentimental existence, would not itself be considered some sort of clutter by the puritanical. She wondered if she was indeed, in all her specialisms, clutter. And how did one declutter having decided that was the case?

What's The View, Like?

Today the question asked by the little black book was '(if you are willing to disclose) what is the name of the block of flats that you live in? (if you do indeed live in a block of flats)'. There was one other man in the shop with me, and he commented on how it was unlikely that the owners would get much feedback on this one, as their clientele tended towards the academic, middle-class crowd who habitually resided outside of places collectively referred to as blocks. He went on to talk some total fucking nonsense about intellectual oppression in East Berlin which left people of an educated status unwilling to live anywhere that brought to mind the term 'bloc' and I stopped listening to him because he seemed like a twat. I looked in the book. He had answered, just above me. He had written an abbreviated version of the smart-arse bullshit he was now relaying to me. I asked him where he lived. He said he lived in Christabel. I was confused and he said it was a block of flats in a group named after the Pankhursts. I wondered why he didn't just write that down. His name badge read 'Angus' and I mentally removed the second consonant in an immature act of revenge for his wasting my time.

I wrote 'Percepeid's Wharf' because I thought that it was funny but I'm not going to tell you why. I blanked the man in the shop until he left. I then, in privacy, checked back on the pages that had been filled in since my last visit. The past few days had been busy. Yesterday: favourite time of year; day before: supermarket used most often; day before that: favourite independent business. And there I stopped.

Around ten o'clock at night, the day before the day before yesterday: an entry surrounded by a jagged exclamation bubble, underlined doubly, arrows pointing towards it. The business mentioned in both the 'before eating' and 'after eating' sections was a book shop. Song Street Books. The handwriting was corpulent – it belonged to the felt tip but had been produced in biro like the other entries. It was somehow thicker though; richer. The name in the appropriate column was 'Fran AKA Mr Cramps'.

I looked at my watch. It was only three p.m. I settled upon Song Street Books as my next destination.

The marvels of technology; I looked it up in the palm of my hand. Only a shortish bus ride. The stop I would get off at was about five minutes away from the shop itself, which sat on a backstreet in a fairly central but unimpressive location. I imagined a tumble-down Dickensian structure overflowing with knowledge.

The internet reckoned the place was open for another four hours so I had plenty of time to go and have a snoop around.

Upon entry I was greeted by a collection of six or seven people in 'University Of Manchester Surfing Society' T-shirts – greeted in the sense that they were there but did not notice me, but I noticed them and stayed to watch for a while. They occupied a clearing surrounded by a curved wall of bookshelves that was broken only by a narrow gap directly opposite the front door and stood side by side, sideways, in rigid formation, arms held out, one in front of them, one behind as they waved their bodies and bobbed slightly, as if they were afloat rather than stood in a book shop. They all had their eyes closed. Every now and again one of them would fall down and, without opening their eyes, the others would shout 'wipeout!' and the fallen person would struggle to their feet again and pretend to climb back onto the board they had just pretended to have pulled back close to them using the supposed leash attached to their left ankle. This happened infrequently, I assumed, what with their T-shirts saying they were the first team. I looked at the books that surrounded us. There was a two for one on items named things like 'The Surfer's Bible' and 'An Appreciation Of Waves' and 'Haynes Surfing Manual' etc. and I supposed that such books do not sell particularly well in Manchester except to poseurs. So the display all clicked and started to make sense in a way that left me feeling a little empty. I left via the narrow gap in the shelf-wall that existed opposite the front door and found myself in a maze of corridors formed by articulately – and yes, I mean to use that adjective but I cannot explain why – arranged shelves, branching off occasionally to lead to more clearings, passages with curtained doorways at the end and in one case, a carefully constructed spiral of shelves: end point unknown.

I picked the spiral, naturally, and followed it to a dead end, retraced my steps without even looking at the books that flanked me, and moved in the direction of one of the curtained doorways. I pulled the paisley rag aside and found myself in an area considerably better lit and immediately free from the noise of the surfers by the entrance. This room was more conventional, the artistic arrangement of shelves evidently being a work in progress that had not reached this far back into the shop. The wallpaper was paisley and a hand-drawn sign read 'Paisley Room' and the first shelf contained books about the Scottish town of the same name. I did not look at these. About three feet to the left of the door through which I had just walked stood a metal ladder, covered in glitter and leading up through a trapdoor. Fastened to the ladder was a sign with an arrow pointing upwards to a picture of a till and I briefly wondered about wheelchairs and then followed the sign. The room directly above 'Paisley Room' resembled an ordinary office in the sense that it had a desk in it and it was a bit soulless. It was barren except for the desk and a shelf, which sat behind two pieces of graffiti drawn roughly onto the wooden floor. The one in front of the desk read 'Desk' and the one in front of the shelf read 'The Shelf'. The Shelf contained a number of books I had not seen before. It took a while, but I eventually clocked that there was somebody behind the desk and so I immediately felt compelled to purchase something. I picked a book from The Shelf and looked at it briefly. Sounded French or something, might be good, who knew. I looked at the man behind the desk. He looked like any old literature student. Perpetually recognisable. I gestured towards the pile of notebooks on the desk and looked at him inquisitively. For Sale? Always come in handy, those. He cocked his head and I picked them up, assuming that was okay.

"Five?"

"Plus three for the book."

"Cool."

"Nice one."

"Double good, or whatever I'm meant to say."

A half smile – he seemed unable to properly engage – distracted or something.

Handed over the cash in pound coins, smiled and backed towards the ladder.

This is impossible, but I'm going to have to tell it this way anyway. I descended the ladder – the same one I had ascended moments earlier – and found myself in somewhere different from 'Paisley Room'. This room was the same size and shape, with the same arrangement of bookshelves, but had different wallpaper, books on display, curtain at the entrance. Either the people who work here are the fastest interior decorators around, or I'm mad, or they are wizards. This room was whitewashed, smelt like burnt toast and contained books exclusively about fire safety. On the end of each shelf was a mirror. I left through the curtain – a Hawaiian sort of print – and found myself back amongst the surfers. Very confusing. I took a right and followed a wide passageway that led away from the surfers and towards a less confusing part of the shop which contained a noticeboard talking about unlikely sounding local events and a door with a handle polished to the point of near-perfect reflection. I pushed open this door and entered a kitchen-type facility – corridor-like in its layout – and at the far end was a door marked 'Private: do come in'. I followed instructions and came across a tent. A voice came from the shadow inside.

"Can't you read the sign? You're running amok. You're running an absolute mok."

"What?"

Ralph crawled out.

"Oh, the actor."

No real trace of surprise. He consulted something behind me, which I would come to realise was a calendar pinned to the door through which I had just entered the room.

"The Ralph."

"That's me. Welcome, I suppose."

"Right."

"I suppose you've come for your payment?"

"Well no, it was cash in..."

"No bother. Here's more." He thrust a couple of twenties into my hand. "It'll air soonish I think. He has a way with these TV scheduling types, somehow. Nobody else seems to. Don't tell anybody."

"I do not know what is going on."

"Yup."

"..."

"Ah, you bought something."

"Yes..."

"Don't show me, I'll immediately forget – part of the job and all."

"Hmmm."

"Precisely. Do you know your way out?"

He moved to the back of the room and pushed the bar on a fire escape door. It said it was alarmed but it evidently wasn't. I left through that door, reeling, and found myself on a backstreet that ran parallel to the one on which the front door was situated. A back-back street. A further-back street.

Serial Surveillance

Ezra was in a room and he was suffering from Kramp. Too much guitar playing recently.

"You see, I had an idea that will direct all attention to me even in the small clubs. Stop the audience from talking over my songs and stuff. I mean, there's plenty of places without live music that they can go to for a chat. So I thought this idea up that I call Directive Serial Surveillance, or DSS, but I'm not sure if that is an appropriate name so it's only a temporary one for now. Anyway, I realised that people do not like being heard, watched, seen, glanced at by people they do not give explicit permission to do so. So they will therefore surely not want their conversations in bars to be overheard or whatever. Especially not by everybody else in the bar, if you follow. Especially not if some of the people in that bar are trying to listen to something else, i.e. the musician. So here's what I've started doing: I'm putting covert microphones in the audience – mics that aren't directional, you know, the ones that pick up a lot of sound from within a reasonably large radius. I've been selling a lot from The Shelf so I've saved up a bit and bought in five, all second hand. Secret ones, like for surveillance. I stick them under beer mats and the like. Then, I start playing, and if somebody tries to talk over me, what happens is that what they are saying is picked up by the microphones and comes out through the PA system.

127

Granted, if everybody clocked on and started yelling, it'd be counterproductive. But rather, what has been happening is that – I imagine mainly because in the majority of cases most people are quiet whilst I am playing – the odd person speaks up and what they say comes out, nice and loud. I always make sure the audience mics are nice and loud. They get really embarrassed and sheepish. When I'm playing a gig and I have a friend in the audience, I enlist the friend to do daggers at anybody who falls into my trap, smiting the guilty talker with the hammer of social judgement. It intensifies the effect of my strategy. Sometimes, somebody else whispers immediately after the first talker has been broadcast, to ask what just happened, or something, and they too come through the PA. They get creeped out – maybe they think the mic I'm singing into is really sensitive or something. They move to the back – which is point one to me as a talker has moved away for starters, but then when they get caught out again, they shut up for good as they start to think they are being watched, or are the butt of some joke or something. I ensure that nobody decides to take advantage and sing along or anything by utilising my evenly dispersed dagger-givers and, if needs be, one of them'll lob a pint over anybody who gets a bit rowdy. But that hasn't been needed yet. Anyway, what I'm saying is basically this form of surveillance ought to ensure that people behave at my gigs. Perhaps I'll allow singing along at some point, but realistically that won't happen as nobody knows my songs. And no, you're wrong, it won't kill the atmosphere. It'll just shut up the gobby pissed couple at the back who aren't really there for music and just want to look sophisticated for a while before they cop off or whatever. People will become paranoid if they think every single thing they say is noted by other people around them – every thought they have or thing they do is somehow noticed or expected by people monitoring their patterns. It's all about patterns and sequences really; typical behaviour when people are subjected to certain stimuli. In this case, the people in question are being made conspicuous. As a result of that they are being noticed and judged in a way they probably do not want. They are therefore going to start to feel uncomfortable and act, predictably, in a manner that means that the attention upon them might eventually either dissipate or at least turn into something not so bad. Like, oh, it was just a one off bit of a natter, they won't do it again. Something like that. Basically, they will shut the fuck up for a bit. It's funny though. When people realise that they are being watched, they start to become so conscious of the way they are behaving that they start to act differently to how they usually would. For example – and I might be putting a lot of thought into a coincidence; I'm not a scientist – but when these people get really conscious that they have been recorded or eavesdropped upon – that their actions are more public and observed than they thought –

they do things I want, without me having to try very hard at all. The first bloke that I did it to: he ended up being the one who cheered loudest, and that was after a song he clearly did not even know.

<u>Personally, I hate it when we watch a film we have already seen simply because we cannot think of something else to do.</u>

"Personally, I hate it when we watch a film we have already seen simply because we cannot think of something else to do."

"Tell me other things you hate."

"I hate it when I get drunk and eat the three remaining packets of Hula Hoops."

"Cool, one more."

"I get pissed off that instead of feeling high I just feel enclosed and words elongate."

"Weed, or what?"

"Yeah, weed."

"Okay. Then brandish the weapon."

"It's a water gun. It looks silly."

"Brandish it."

"Okay. Facial expressions?"

"Blank. Pious."

"Like this?"

"Yes. That's right."

"They won't even see it with this balaclava on."

"..."

"And why exactly will this look good or do whatever it is that you want it to do?"

"It's a parody."

"Of what?"

"You'll see when it's done."

"Can I take this off? I have a warm face."

"Yes. We're done now. Kramps will be good with this; actually wait, hang on, put that spoon in your mouth – yes – through the mouth hole – yes – hold it there – yes – we'll green screen the rest. Nice one."

"Can I say that I occasionally smoke weed on television? I'll need a proper career and stuff at some point."

"You're hidden."

"Yeah, oh right."

"Besides, you can just say you're acting anyway."

Ralph extracted the tape of grainy footage and stuck it in one of his cavernous pockets. No 'cheers Ezra'. Still, bit of paid work: not too bad. Some sort of thing where we were filming us pretending to film something else that was far removed from what it was that we were actually filming; only it wasn't because it was a parody that brought it all back into the realm of the relatable through the insertion of everyday items. Or some shit like that. A follow up to the latest controversy. I wondered whom they thought they were targeting. I wondered if Ralph was still aware that he was supposed to be running a book shop; a responsibility that had basically fallen to me by default due to his absence.

Speaking of which, something interesting – sort of – took place during my last shift in the shop. I was bored, as is usual when I'm at work, but I was making the time pass by pretty quickly. I might even venture so far as to suggest that I was making it pass by faster than I usually manage to make it pass.

Anyway, I was making the time whizz on by so that I could get off and go and meet Bill that evening over at The Castle and the bloody window cleaner fell in on me. It was a good job I wasn't up to anything, to be honest. Anyway, he fell in and his face was a total mess but I couldn't help it, I laughed. Sort of out of shock, I suppose. But the window cleaner was a mess and he seemed pretty pissed off. I assume this was because he realised that it was unlikely that he'd get paid now that he'd smashed the whole window through. I wonder how he managed to do that.

Back to the story: Ralph had been on the phone. He turned to me, looking pleased with himself.

"Okay, Kramps likes my idea. He reckons it could work, if we green screen you on top of some high building. So we've got to get you ascending some stairs or something."

"Cool."

"Backwards, and really, really quickly."

"That's hard."

"No, because we'll video you running, tumbling down them, and reverse it."

"Clever clever."

"That an insult?"

"Knowledge is power."

"Whatever. We'll film it this week."

The power to reverse reality, only something like two minutes after it has happened, all within the confines of a small, electronic box, is, like, really cool. And then to tag it onto something else, something else that happened a few days earlier, and make it look like they both happened within minutes of one another (as long as you have the same clothes/haircut/spots etc.) never ceases to amaze me. Yes, it's old hat. Yes, people have wondered about this kind of thing tonnes before. But still, allow me my meagre attempt at philosophical(?) thought every once in a while. I'm no tech-head.

About three weeks later and what we'd filmed still had not been shown to me. I had no idea what it was that they were doing to or with it. I had barely seen Ralph since the filming and reversing on the stairs. I had no gigs booked, so basically I just filled my time hanging around the shop in the vain hope that I might sell one of these bastards off The Shelf so I could earn a bit of extra cash from my increasingly negligent boss.

Last time I was in the shop, though, feet up on the desk, in my bare 'office', I was peckish. Honestly, this is the most interesting part of my life I have to tell you about at the moment – my eating schedule. Anyway, I got hungry, so I set about trying to find some food and, naturally, popped inside Ralph's tent room and had a poke around his over-full cubby holes and ex-bathrooms that are dotted around the room's perimeter. One of them was full of boxes of that weird cereal that I learned Ralph was somehow so involved with back when we ran that errand on that weird day at that factory place. Anyway, I picked up the box – I'd never actually looked at it before really – and read the logo and the ingredients and the pictures on the front. Sometimes people say that such things are the last bastion of literature. The only place that true original thought and unadulterated, subtly misleading fiction can continue to exist. I don't really know what those people are talking about. It was boring. Orangey-amber-or-something-eye-catching-and-sort-of-homely-like-that. Fireside-commodity-chic. What am I on about? A character on the front I do not care to remember. Lots of exclamation marks. Nothing negative. The weird stylised vowel near the end. An advertisement for a vaguely interesting free gift that promised to be tacky. I took the box and headed back up to my desk and, once I had got there, remembered that I would need a bowl and spoon.

These were eventually located alongside Ralph's television, unwashed, and I moved towards the functioning plumbing that existed elsewhere and washed them with hand soap. Clean enough.

Finally I was equipped. The bowl was set on the desk, which had not been restocked since we were cleaned out of those pretentious branded notebooks some time ago. I dropped the spoon in it, so that it would fill up naturally as I filled the bowl with cereal. Two birds, one stone, and everything like that. I poured the cereal in. I did not want to use milk. A plastic, orange package landed in my bowl as it became half full.

Naturally, I tore it open. The thrill of a surprise never quite leaves you. Inside was your usual tat. A viewfinder, this time. Or whatever they're called. You look into it and see a picture, you flick something, you get another picture. Only, typical tat, this one didn't flick. Why the fuck anybody would want to 'collect them all' as per the instruction on the packaging I do not know. I looked into it and was disappointed. A couple, serving fish and chips. Maybe it was some sort of modern – and totally disappointing – take on 'Happy Families'. Mr and Mrs Cheap the chip shop owners. Something like that. Anyway, I was unimpressed, so I threw the viewfinder into the desk drawer I reserve for shit that I can sift through when notably bored, and got stuck in to my dry cereal.

Collections

A collection collected; an obsession put to bed. An obsession of hers, to have got one of each, to have filled everything out, to have heard, seen or touched all of what there was on offer. It drove the man crazy, but now that their book was totally full she was allowing them to act.

They had amassed an enormous amount of data most people would not want. Months of collecting and noting, of carefully removing and replacing rubber gloves; unfeasible dexterity demanded of him under the pressure synonymous with the catering industry. She criticised the odd grease stain on an important page, but was generally satisfied. They had enough information.

There was a record playing. It was playing because it was relevant. The first thing they had done with the data was search through it for names they recognised, so that they could see if there was any sort of celebrity clout behind their supposedly academic piece of work. It was potentially likely – they had inadvertently garnered something of a reputation for the standard of food served at the chip shop that was the front for their experiment.

The woman walked over to the record player and broke protocol, putting her finger against the vinyl to stop it spinning, just to look, once again, at the picture on the label. It was this piece of art – replicated on the sleeve of the record also, but only after you scratched away a silvery surface with a coin (a measure enforced by shops to hide the offensive cover) – that had made them so excited to see that part of the band name was present in their book. A shared proper noun. A man in their book had signed 'Ezra Scarlatti'.

The record they were listening to was by a band called The Scarlatti Tilt. Named after the mind-blowing Richard Brautigan story; a fact the press were often eager to highlight. Noteworthy because the record had achieved a reasonable degree of popularity due to its appearance – pre-addition of the silvery stuff – in local record shops. Noteworthy because, although it was released on an unknown label and was by a band that had until then gone totally unnoticed, its artwork alone earned it airplay on stations attempting to be controversial.

The people in the band had remained elusive; indeed, since the record's release, no gigs had taken place by anybody using the moniker The Scarlatti Tilt. Articles called them 'reclusive'. Rumour hinted at a few solo shows by various members of the band. Somebody mentioned the sitar player being arrested; anotherbody claimed to have met the bass player working as a runner on an advertisement shoot. Very few people claimed to have seen the band live before the record was released. Those who did gave unlikely tales of gigs in rooms with malfunctioning smoke machines that obscured the performers, or even shows in 'total, pitch darkness'. Nobody really knew what any of the band members looked like. It was all conceited bollocks. Hackneyed attempts at mystique. Surely it wouldn't work the next time the band tried it? Sometimes it's nice to feel like you know what's going on, for once. But openness doesn't allow for the competitive knowledge-offs so popular in the art world.

There had been a few radio interviews with people who were supposedly part of the band, all rumoured to have been given using false voices; perhaps using false names also. But it was the recollection of a disastrous radio interview with a member of the band going by the name Ezra that prompted the couple's excitement. It all added up. It seemed to be too much of a coincidence. Surely it was worth a shot.

Their first port of call was the radio station on which the interview had taken place. The woman rang up the station and received the information that the interview in question had been done on the evening show, with a DJ named Bill. The station's flagship bollocks-natterer and something of an expert on whatever it was cool to be an expert on at any given time. The couple masqueraded as some sort of vague talent-agency-cum-promo-company and were able to wrangle this Bill's phone number, in a manner the woman suspected was not completely above board. Needless to say, such an element of shadiness only made the whole thing more exciting.

Upon ringing this Bill character they became familiar with a drunken and entirely accommodating voice on the other end, which garrulously informed them that they ought to come over to his house right away if they wanted to meet what he might be inclined to call 'the real deal'. They asked for an address and were given one on the other side of town, two bus rides away. Bill seemed confident that things would still be happening by the time they reckoned they could get there, so they left the house and made their way to the bus stop at the end of the road. They expected to arrive at Bill's in about an hour.

Bill's house was in fact a flat. The television took centre stage in the living room, decorated with crumpled beer cans, the screen slick with something unknowable. The space was full and depressingly male. The man wandered, typically, kitchenwards and helped himself to a bottle of something syrupy and started to look around. He had no idea what he was looking for. After a moment of thought, he decided that whomever it was that was the centre of attention ought to be the first point of reference. Presumably DJs kept up their role of entertaining people en masse outside of working hours.

The man and the woman split up and set about meeting people.

The man made his way to the doorway of the kitchen, pushing past a person restringing a violin whilst talking to a skinny youth in a Trout Mask Replica T-shirt. The building was swelling with wasted noise. He spotted the woman speaking to a sweaty bloke with blonde hair that reached his neckline. Standing at the doorway between the kitchen and the living room the man noticed that the centre of the room was completely empty. Standard fare: furniture pushed to the edges, etc. But nobody occupied the space, either. People gathered in clusters around the room's perimeter – a few stood on the slice of balcony, smoking – discussing things in a manner which the man supposed they thought made them look intellectual. He did not catch much of the conversation that was going on around him; he was too busy trying to find the centre of attention, an extremely difficult task when one is not willing to direct one's own attention wholeheartedly to any specific source of entertainment for fear of missing another. At one point somebody said something about somebody doing something that was 'radically different' – not the usual thing that you encounter at a party. The person was totally thrilled about such a prospect and even mentioned that somebody might actually grow as a person as a result of whatever this forthcoming event was to be. Everybody was wearing a T-shirt that was a reference to something else. They seemed to get progressively more obscure as the man moved his gaze clockwise around the place, trying to get each one. The room was a wall, really. Impenetrable.

The wall was saturated in booze. There was little collective knowledge as to what it was that was actually going on. In the far left corner the telephone where the woman's voice had previously existed stood atop a small side table. There was a ruckus in the kitchen and out stumbled the man with the now-strung violin, followed by the Captain Beefheart fan. Everybody quietened down in a way that the man was not entirely comfortable with. The guy with the violin looked like a young David Byrne. All eyes were on him, so the man's search for a centre of attention was finally satisfied. He decided to approach the violin player at the next opportunity and ask him who was who in this place. The Byrne-a-like started to scrape at the strings with effort, seemingly with the intention of squeezing a wince from the wall of beer-soaked feigned impassivity towards which he was playing. He got none. Even those who had heralded the event with hushed, inflated chatter now looked to the ground and adopted a nonchalant lean towards the nearest solid object, animate or otherwise. The man carried on regardless, scraping away with his frayed bow and occasionally looking towards Beefheart Fan for what seemed like guidance. Beefheart Fan would occasionally nod approvingly and sip from his bottle of Buckfast. The man would continue to scrape with gusto following these sporadic suggestions of encouragement.

"Well this is a bit fucking vaudeville, isn't it."

A disconnected voice that struck the nail on the head, as far as the man was concerned. He wasn't even sure if that made sense, but it made sense to him. If this was supposed to be some sort of avant-garde climax to the party he was almost overwhelmingly underwhelmed, if that was possible. A long-limbed man in round spectacles stood beside him staring at the floor and pushing his thumbs in and out of his belt loops. He caught the man's eye and grimaced, as if to apologise but not quite going that far. Long-limbs turned his gaze to the violinist and squinted. The man looked up at the ceiling for want of anything better to do and waited in that position until his neck hurt.

A voice at his shoulder. It was high-pitched and a little husky. He didn't recognise it, but he liked it. He turned.

"Bit of a shit party, eh?"

"Yes."

"All a bit focused on what it wants to be rather than what it is."

"Spot on."

"I mean, a fucking violin? Come on. That isn't even cliché. It sort of transcends that and becomes something even worse."

"Exactly, like something so opposed to cliché that it is itself cripplingly predictable, but mainly because of its self-conscious unpredictability."

"I sort of get what you mean, but I fear that you are at risk of doing that which you criticise."

"..."

"Winding you up, don't worry."

"Okay"

"Was talking to Beefheart over there. He says he recognises you. Says he saw you in a viewfinder. Like, a freebie out of cereal or something. I reckon he's been smoking."

"Chocofix?"

"Don't know. He just said it."

"My wife collects them. I think she'd have recognised me."

"It's hard to spot yourself, sometimes."

"..."

"Look around. This is a veritable hotbed for people blind to themselves."

"..."

"Honestly." A smile.

"Alright."

"What?"

"Alright, as in, okay."

"Taciturn."

"Yup."

She paused for a few seconds, during which time the man returned his gaze to the stained ceiling.

"He can't even play the violin."

"You know, I think that might actually be the point, for some reason."

"I can't stand people learning to play the violin."

"Hmmm."

The man desperately wanted what was going

on to stop. The entire gathering was focused on the peculiar performance. He thought parties were supposed to be fun. Instead, he felt like he had done when he had, out of sympathy, agreed to go to an 'immersive experience' his friend had put on while studying for an art degree down in London.

Let's try and have fun. Let me go.

There was a shouted 'fuck this' and then all hope of establishing any sort of connection with anybody new was dashed. Dashed by a water gun. The woman stormed in, apparently no longer bothered about their research project, armed with a plastic, revolver-shaped thing. The man had no idea where she got it from. And water left the tank and entered the atmosphere.

The poor violinist was soaked.

Nobody intervened.

The man started to dance and tried to reject the overriding sensation that he was existing amongst an ecstatic failure. The soaked violinist had been replaced by Something that he recognised spinning against the needle and he was happy for now. The woman had been politely asked to leave after the incident, but he was aware that she would hold a taxi for them – defying financial concerns – for at least the next half hour. He had time. He was dancing opposite T-shirt Beefheart, who was leaning in and muttering something into his ear about a piece of artwork that he was somehow involved with: the man had forgotten to care.

Outside he found her holding the taxi door open. The meter read upwards of thirty pounds. The taxi hadn't even been moving. Bastard.

"We should have got the morning bus. I could've killed some more time in there."

"Did you find him?"

"…"

"…"

"Oh, yeah, no, don't think so."

"Then this was a waste of time."

"At points it was fun, though. Wasn't it?"

"…"

<u>Guilt Rings</u>

Jenny was visiting her dad again. He had been asleep when she had arrived, and he remained that way. So Jenny went in search of something to read on his bookcase.

Idly fingering through the rows, she came across something which intrigued her. Vertically, it had the title first:

G
U
I
L
T

R
I
N
G
S

And then it had the author's name:

F
R
A
N
K

C
R
U
M
P

It was narrow. About twenty pages thick. Hardback, so that the front and back covers tapped together when you closed the book.

There was no sign of a date of publication. She considered putting it back, but instead pocketed it. That night, having gone home without managing to wake her father once during her visit, she read it.

Ch. 1

The smoke from the previous evening had taken up residence in his clothes, and he smelt it as he rode across the flats beyond the pier. The tide was out and it was mumbling something nobody cared to understand.

A woman was teaching her dog to swim, it seemed, and as he passed her, wheels digging into the sand that was softening with the sun, she got a quick blast of the music that was playing from the speaker strapped to the back of his seat.

She didn't think people rode choppers anymore, and then she went back to her dog.

If you had been sitting out on the shallow dunes of the old golf course just north-east of Nairn on that Tuesday morning, and had been doing so for a few hours, you would probably have some idea as to where the smoke-soaked boy was going.

He had been preceded, huffily, by a scrawny counterpart laden with a wooden boat, which he dragged, rope over his shoulder, through the shallows. He had been trying to move faster than was possible in the circumstances.

The smoke-soaked boy was running late. The two dots he could make out near to where the sand stopped were most likely what he was heading for. The larger of the two dots was bobbing, the other no doubt trying to control this.

A bicycle had been a poor choice. The rucksack hung from the handlebars, a permanent threat to the wellbeing of the front spokes, bulging with the contents of the smoke-soaked boy's mum's fridge, which had been, as usual, a scaled-down replica of the lager section in the supermarket.

He hoped that the cans wouldn't be missed.

The smaller of the two dots would probably be annoyed by the smoke-soaked boy's tardiness. They had meticulously planned this, down to the minute, and he'd spoiled it.

"Do you have any clue what fucking time it is?"

These were the words which greeted him when he finally, after years and years and years, made it to the two dots. The larger dot had been a boat all along, and the other dot was Willard, and always had been. Not much had changed after all that time.

Willard was knee-deep and held the rocking boat with his left arm. It had an old outboard and two oars lay along the bottom, underneath the two benches. A few carrier bags sat in the bow, and Willard took the rucksack from the front of the chopper and threw it in with them.

"Can I put my bike in?"

"Go on."

They hauled the bike up and waded into the sea, careful to avoid splashing any salt water onto the rusting frame.

"What's in the rucksack?"

"Stella, mainly. Mum's stuff."

"I've got my fishing things."

"I'm sorry I'm late, Willard."

Ch. 2

They climbed into the boat, soaking the benches with their wet jeans as they sat down, Willard by the outboard, Smoke near the bags. Underneath the front bench was a rolled up tarpaulin, wrapped around three tent poles. They were going to use it as a canopy.

As Willard pulled the starting cord on the outboard he asked Smoke what his excuse for getting out of school had been, and then he remembered that he probably hadn't needed one. Smoke didn't answer, instead staring out to the sea and wondering where Willard was going to take them. The only decision made in advance about their day from this point onwards was north.

"I'm glad that we're finally doing this."

"Yeah, like the dads."

"Yeah. It's been a long time."

There was very little evidence of life out there, on that day. A few seagulls, buoys, things that Smoke guessed were lobster pots. The water was calm, but Smoke still kept checking to make sure that the disposable barbecue was safely within its cocoon of plastic bags. They made their way out until they could no longer see the shore, cut the motor and let themselves drift. They had all day to get back. It was coming up to what felt like time to eat.

Willard strapped a snorkelling mask to his face and unbuttoned his corduroy shirt and took it off. He leant over the side of the boat and pushed his face into the water. His thick fringe floated on the surface and he stayed submerged until he was forced to come up, gasping.

"Too murky. I can't see anything."

Smoke passed his friend the fishing things. Willard set about getting started on that and Smoke guessed that he had better make himself busy with something. It seemed like a good time to get the barbecue lit, while everything was calm. He fished around in his pocket for a lighter and peeled the packaging from the barbecue with his other hand. He lit the paper that covered the coals and put the barbecue on one of the benches, near the raised edge of the boat. He then pulled the tarpaulin from underneath him and slid the poles out from inside the roll.

"Here."

Willard put down the fishing things and took two poles and shoved them into brackets they had fastened into the two back corners of the boat. Smoke did the same with the third and a bracket in the middle, between the two benches. He then unrolled the tarpaulin and draped it over the poles, casting a shadow over Willard. They both reached up to the top of different poles and asked the other where the gaffa tape was. Smoke bent down and found it in one of the carrier bags and stuck his end of the tarpaulin to his pole. He threw the tape to Willard, who secured the other two poles and they both sat down again.

The barbecue was probably going to take a long time to heat up. Smoke rummaged around in his bag and managed to release a four-pack from the tangle. He pulled one from its plastic ring and passed it to Willard, who thanked him. Willard could never steal beer because his parents never drank. Smoke separated his own from the pack and opened it, taking a sip. He pulled a face, but looked away from his friend as he did so. Willard had done the same, and they were both facing opposite directions when they resolved to put on more of a performance next time.

"Good beer."

"Just what I needed."

"Perfect on a day like this."

The fishing stuff lay on the floor, no longer of interest despite it supposedly being the reason they were there. The bike was getting in the way in between the two benches where they wanted to put their feet, so Smoke set about moving it to the bow, and dumping the bags in the middle. They'd need to access these more often anyway, so it made sense to have them closer to hand.

Smoke decided to lie back on his bench and stare up at the canopy. He thought about the sky. The way that people would sometimes say that they were surrounded by blue when they were at sea and under clear skies was nonsense. The sea was not blue today. The sky was blotchy, at points. It was easy to look in any direction and find something that was not blue. Willard was staring into the barbecue and looked to be thinking of something to say, but Smoke wanted him to know that there was no pressure. They had known each other long enough to stay quiet for a bit.

Smoke took a sip of his beer, nearly emptying it over himself as he tilted it too steeply while drinking. He sat up and drank the rest and opened another. He took off his shirt and threw it up onto the top of the canopy for it to dry in the sun. Willard said something about it being blown off but Smoke licked his finger and held it up in the air and said he wasn't too worried about that. It was an old shirt anyway.

He lay back down again. A seagull shat onto the chopper, the shit landing on the speaker of the large old-fashioned radio. It would be a bastard trying to get that out of the speaker grills, Smoke thought.

Willard and Smoke had known one another since they were less than one. Willard's father had treated Smoke's mother soon after Smoke was born, and whilst that was taking place, Willard's mother had basically brought the two boys up together. They'd had the occasional fight, but never anything serious. As is often the case, these things were forgotten as soon as something else worth bothering with came along.

One thing Willard did not know about Smoke was that he had never had a girlfriend. This was a dark secret; the truth buffered by a series of vague lies told roughly once a year when Willard started pressing the issue, wondering why he'd never met any of Smoke's elusive lovers. The story Smoke always went with was that he was something of a Lothario whenever he was in Dorset on a family holiday.

Willard was the genuine success story and Smoke was, on the surface of things, happy to play second fiddle.

"You think we're drifting far?"

"Can you see if we are?"

"Not much to judge it by, really."

Smoke craned his neck and tried to look around him without sitting up. It didn't work. He sat up. Land was not visible and existed only as a memory for both of them. Willard went over to the motor and started it.

"Turn around and go back a bit, so we're never too far from the start."

"Okay."

He turned the boat round and they spent ten minutes going back the way they had come.

"Isn't it funny how being in a boat is basically the opposite of being in a bath?"

"What?"

"Lying down in a space that has no water in it, surrounded by water in all places outside of the space."

"Oh, right."

Willard asked for one of Smoke's mum's cigarettes and lit it and breathed in and coughed.

Willard remembered the days before what his family called the 'big turnaround'. His dad lying face down in the bath. You could see the dead skin on the bottom of his feet, whitened by the time in the water. Pulling him up and out and asking him what he was doing. Willard had strong opinions on whether or not a person below the age of fifteen should know what it feels like to bear the full weight of one of their parents.

He tried again on the cigarette, determined to try and make it work. It didn't and he spat it out into the cluttered hull. He asked Smoke for another beer and tried to work out how far they'd drifted since they had last cut out the motor.

Smoke was lying down again, and moved only his arm in the vague direction of the bags in response to his friend's request. Willard watched, and started to direct the blind arm towards its target. Smoke followed the instructions until he touched something metallic and pulled on it. The canopy fell down. Now forced to get up, Smoke placed the pole back into its bracket and looked properly for the beer.

He found one and opened it for himself without thinking.

"That radio get signal out here?"

"It's got shit in it now."

"Try it."

"But it's got shit in it from that seagull."

"Which seagull?"

"One from before. I didn't mention it at the time."

"Try it anyway."

Smoke pulled the radio off the back of his bike and tried to tune it. He pulled the aerial up and pointed it out from under the canopy. He fiddled with the dial but he couldn't get anything.

"I wonder what fishermen do when they're out here for days on end?"

"Don't listen to the radio, I guess."

"Better make sure that it doesn't get wet, actually. Keep it under here."

"It doesn't look like rain."

"Spray though, maybe, if the sea gets rougher."

"Doesn't look like it will."

"Just in case though. It would be a shame to get it wet and break it."

"I'm not sure that would happen, but okay."

It was a strange argument and Smoke didn't really know why he hadn't just done what Willard had suggested straight away. Some sort of desire to make sure his friend knew he had ideas of his own? Some kind of insecurity that flared up whenever he feared somebody was making a better suggestion than the one he had made? Willard was his best friend, but Smoke guessed that part of him wanted to make sure he was better than Willard at some things. To assert his value, for whatever reason. Smoke didn't know.

Willard had picked the fishing rod back up and cast into the sea. He gaffa taped the end of the rod to the bench and left it there, propped against the rim of the boat, with half an eye on it to see if anything bit.

"Hey Willard, I've had this idea."

"This idea about what?"

"For a story, or something, maybe."

"What is it?"

"It's about this guy who has died. A guy who has hanged himself."

"Oh, okay."

"And they cut him down and take his clothes off for an autopsy or something and there's this tattoo on his torso. On his chest and on his belly."

"Right."

"A big tattoo."

"What is the tattoo of?"

"A shopping list. It's the shopping list for the next day."

"Why?"

"So his family know what they need to get the next day."

"Yes, I get that bit, but why."

"I don't know really. It's just an idea I had."

Realising that he had not yet provided for his friend, Smoke pulled the last can out of the four-pack they were on and passed it to Willard, who had just stuffed his empty inside one of the carrier bags. He then found another four-pack and ripped a can for himself out of it. He had drained his previous one quickly, ignoring the taste.

The barbecue looked to be getting hot enough to cook.

"You want food?"

"Go on."

Willard found some sausages in the bag which had been warming as the sun climbed to its zenith for the day. They smelt alright, though. He took them out of the packet and gave them to Smoke, who stuck sharpened sticks into them and put them on the barbecue. They'd be ready pretty soon.

They both looked out of the boat and were quiet for a long time. The sausages spat at their legs as they heated up. There were not many clouds and those that were there were wispy; not worth speaking about. Not that they ever spoke about clouds anyway. Willard sneezed and slurped the beer from the top of the can where he had sloshed it.

"Do you feel a bit drunk yet?"

"No, not really, I don't think."

Lies. But better to say no than risk the truth. The rod was ineffably still, not even the gentle movement of the sea seemed to be disturbing it. There would be no fish, it seemed.

And then the gaffa tape lost its hold on the wooden bench and the rod jerked out of place, knocking one of the poles. The pole's unstable position in the makeshift bracket was destabilised, and the canopy fell down again. The barbecue was knocked to the floor where it was extinguished by the dampness of the wood. It had landed upside down depositing an ashy sludge at their feet. And into the ash rolled the half-cooked sausages.

"Oh fucking hell," they both said, not quite in unison.

"..."

"We've still got crisps."

"Help me put the canopy back up."

"We'll have to scrape that up."

"Get a carrier bag. Make it the rubbish receptacle. Put all our shit in it."

"Empty the stuff from that one into that one. Does the one you're emptying have any holes in the bottom? I'll use the cardboard packaging to shovel the ash in."

"Yep, no holes."

"Good. Okay, hold it there."

"..."

"Done. May as well put all the cans into it as well."

By now the rod had drifted away but Willard did not seem particularly bothered. Smoke had raised the issue and he had just shrugged and said it wasn't his best one anyway. It was a shame that they wouldn't catch any fish, though.

Smoke and Willard began searching around the boat for the cans they had shoved into various nooks so as to stop them rolling around. This took a few minutes because both of them were absolutely certainly not feeling drunk yet. They put them into the carrier bag designated as rubbish receptacle. Willard asked for another beer. Smoke reached over to the rucksack and pulled out the three beers, held together by their plastic rings. He separated two and put the remaining one, with its plastic rings dangling from it, back into the rucksack. Willard watched him and then looked around the floor of the boat. He started to poke around inside the rubbish bag.

"You got the plastic thing from the first four-pack?"

"What?"

"The plastic ring thing. You got it? I can't find it in the bin."

"No. I'm not sure what I did with it. We've been moving about a fair bit. Could have knocked it out of the boat?"

Willard looked worried.

"Mate, that's not great, really. Those things are bad things to just let go like that."

Smoke shrugged and looked out to sea. The sun was reflecting into his eyes. There was a fair current. They'd probably drifted a long way since they drank that first four-pack. Willard was still looking at him, worried. This seemed to bother him.

"Animals get stuck in them. Seriously. You're fucking up the wellbeing of the sea when you let things like this happen."

"I didn't even see it happen. It's not like I chucked it."

"The fish don't know that."

"What?"

"As far as the fish are concerned you may as well have chucked it. The same end result."

"Fish don't think that much, I'm sure."

"It's bad to let those plastic rings get left in the sea."

"Okay, I'll take more care in future."

"How long have we been out here?"

"Don't know. Around three hours."

"The sea's gentle. We can't have drifted that far."

"Okay."

"Let's go and find it. We have to."

Cosmo sat in the bath that day, staring at his wrinkled genitals as some belly button fluff left its resting place and floated past them, towards the taps.

He twitched his foot and watched his bollocks bob in the water as it moved slightly and thought about work and about family and about the garden. He whispered and listened to his voice cut through the still room – only two o'clock in the afternoon; everybody still at work and school. He looked through the open bathroom door and out across the landing, through the window and watched the rain.

He wondered how he was supposed to bring up his son when he had no idea what a good example was. He wondered whether he had the right to tell anyone off or to tell anyone what to do. He tried to second guess why the people who held him in high regard did so and he fretted over the uncertainty in his mind as to what other people thought of him. He didn't think he deserved much of what he had.

His mind wandered to his pets and he had wished he could just release them all without being labelled a loony. He had no idea where this thought came from, but supposed it was just an irreverent desire to do something frowned upon for the sake of it. He had never really, publicly, done something frowned upon.

The bath water had become lukewarm but he could not summon the energy to get out of it. He tried to twist the plug release with his feet so the water would run out and force him to get up. His feet slipped from the round metal and he gave up. He was stuck there, forever, in a gradually cooling bath on a Tuesday afternoon when he should have been at work. A fucking Tuesday, too.

The telephone rang and he had been about to shout for somebody to answer it when he remembered that he was alone. He let it ring out. Nobody had left a message. The rain had stopped and now it was just one of those usual highland days not worth remembering. Soon everybody would come home and ask questions and be nice and he just really couldn't be bothered with all of that. He was interested, he genuinely was, just not always, and not on that day.

A plane flew overhead, barely audible but visible through the landing window. Probably full of middle-aged American men coming over to try the whisky and ask questions to which they didn't understand the answers and think that they were impressing their wives with how much they could pretend to know. Their bored children would trail round behind them wondering at what age it was that drink stopped just being something to get you pissed. Not that they would know anything about that, anyway, being the age they were and American. Cosmo thought that there were two ways of viewing alcohol: as a drink and as a drug.

He heard the neighbours' car pull into their driveway. A faint flicker of lights going off – they drove a Volvo – and the slam of doors. Bickering, rustling of carrier bags, a struggle to remember who had the keys, more bickering, Ellery had the keys, after all that time, and they were inside.

Cosmo did not want to ever be anything like Alice and Ellery. He wanted to be the furthest possible thing from Alice and Ellery, whatever that happened to be. He was not fussy. That was his only criteria.

About a year earlier Cosmo had read one of those 'kooky' filler stories in the local newspaper. It had been an interview with a local psychic who claimed to be in contact with a particularly nomadic black guillemot which had come up from the Isle of May on a holiday. It was fluent in English, and spoke with the expected accent, the psychic had said. It had been particularly vocal about the state of the seas, the psychic had said. The psychic had told the newspaper that the black guillemot was male and had introduced himself as Robert Palmer. Robert Palmer had said that if he liked it in the area, he might settle down. At least while he was young. A family was, according to the psychic, not something that Robert Palmer was particularly bothered about having at that point in his life. Cosmo did not like the local newspaper. He no longer took it.

Cosmo sighed and stared up at the ceiling and started to realise how cold he was becoming. He knocked the hot tap with his foot in the hope that there was some warm water left but there was not. A gush of cold water hit his foot and he knocked the tap back off again. He still did not get out, though.

Ch. 6

Transcript from interview number forty-three, recorded only an hour ago, in the third year of telepathic correspondence between Charles Hunterville Esquire and Mr Robert Palmer: black guillemot.

Information passed from the mind of RP, to the mind of CH, and out through the mouth of CH into a Dictaphone of unknown origin picked up in a Manchester branch of Maplin last October.

Starts here.

—

CH: Hello Robert Palmer, are you there?

RP: Yes. I'm travelling though, so forgive me if I lose connection every now and again.

CH: That is fine. Thank you for taking the time to talk to me again. What would you like to tell me about this time?

RP: I know that I may tell you this a lot: a bird's-eye view, is what I suppose I am getting, all of the time.

CH: You do say that an awful lot. Almost every time we speak.

RP: And it was with this gift that, today, just now, I saw the most peculiar sight.

CH: Go on, I'm listening.

RP: Is your connection clear?

CH: Yes.

RP: Right. Well I was flying off the coast, over near the old golf course. You know the place?

CH: Yes.

RP: Okay, well I was a fair way out to sea, but the old golf course is a good point to use to give you a vague idea of where I was.

CH: I see.

RP: There was a boat. Only a small one. With a sort of tent in the back half of it, and two people in it. Along with the two people was a bike and a large amount of luggage.

CH: Fishermen?

RP: Well that's what I originally thought, but they were moving far too fast to be fishing.

CH: Travelling to a point where they could fish?

RP: Trust me Charles. I know my fishing. They were in a perfectly good spot. They could have stopped anywhere. And

I followed them. They were travelling for a while, in what I could perceive to be as close to a straight line as humanly possible in a craft of that size when under the influence of currents and air resistance and the like.

CH: Sailing?

RP: No. An outboard. It was under the tent thing but I could hear it. They were taking it in turns to drive, with the other acting as a kind of lookout. The lookout was stood out front, near the bike.

CH: What were they looking for?

RP: Well I don't know. They were almost chasing something. Making a beeline, so to speak.

CH: Did you get a closer look or anything? Something must've happened to make you choose to talk about this.

RP: (The sound of laboured inhalation, followed by coughing and retching noises.)

CH: Robert Palmer?

RP: (The noises continue.)

CH: Robert Palmer? Are you okay?

RP: Sorry, yes. I inhaled an insect or something as I was flying along. No time to dodge it. I'm moving pretty fast, you see. Got to get back to the nest and do my accounts before I decide whether or not I can afford to replace my boiler.

CH: Fair enough. I was wondering if you could tell me more about these two fellows in the boat you saw. I assume there was a reason for you bringing it up?

RP: Yes, there was a reason.

CH: Well, what was it?

RP: I wanted to tell you what I saw when I followed them, obviously. Isn't that rather blatant?

CH: Well, you stopped speaking, that's all.

RP: That's because I inhaled that fucking fly. How do you expect me to speak to you about people in a boat when I'm choking so hard my feathers are loosening, you stupid prick?

CH: Sorry Robert Palmer. Do go on. I know you are doing me a favour by speaking to me.

RP: Fine. I'll tell you what I was going to tell you all along.

CH: Thank you. And sorry.

RP: Apology accepted. Is the signal still clear?

CH: Clear as a bell.

RP: Good. I was following them as they moved in a vague south-easterly direction; I assume retracing their steps or something. Naturally, I thought that they must have dropped something, or remembered something they had seen that they wanted to go back to. I went a bit lower to try and get an idea of the things they were saying, but the general sea noise was causing me a few problems. So I did something that you will probably tell me off for doing.

CH: Go ahead.

RP: I turned on my telepathic skills and picked up their conversation from inside their brains before they said what they said.

CH: How did you make sure you were picking up what they said, and not getting any of it confused with unspoken thoughts?

RP: I have a journalistic background. You know that. I pieced it all together by taking into account the context.

CH: Clever, but you are right. I am a little annoyed. That's quite invasive of you, really, Robert Palmer.

RP: I know, but if I hadn't done it we'd have literally nothing to talk about today. The boiler problems have kept me indoors most of the time lately, faffing about with the pilot light and whatnot. At least I have something to say to you now I went and did that.

CH: Very true. Do go on.

RP: I must say, upon hearing their plight, I became rather attached to the two of them.

CH: Yes?

RP: Yes. You see, they proved to be young men of stellar moral standing. The situation was as follows. They were out skipping school and drinking beers in the boat. They'd suffered a barbecue-related disaster and so were drinking on near-empty stomachs. In what I can only assume was the madness that followed, one of the plastic things that holds beers together in groups of four had fallen out of the boat and into the sea. This caused great distress, especially on the part of the blonde, better-looking one. He had insisted on going and searching for it and had been met with a small amount of resistance from the other boy. However this soon subsided and they set out looking for this thing, resolving to keep looking until they had found it. Naïve, I must say, but a nice enough sentiment. I felt inclined to help them if I could, however, I was well aware that some people – those not as enlightened as yourself, good Charlie – might be somewhat surprised by a talking black guillemot.

CH: A fair assumption, albeit one that reflects the narrow-mindedness of our times.

RP: Quite. Hang on. Let me adjust my goggles.

CH: Done?

RP: Yes. Digging into my eye sockets, they were. I started wearing them recently as I was often finding myself dazzled by the sun setting on summer evenings. These are tinted, you see. UV protection and all that.

CH: Nice.

RP: Handy. Anyway, I had resolved to help them and therefore needed to come up with a way in which I could do so without causing a major stir. I already got some unwanted attention – our whole species did – after that article you had in the local paper couple of years ago. Really not necessary, that, Charlie, as I have so often said since.

CH: Yes, sorry about that.

RP: Anyway, I decided that I must help them find this discarded piece of plastic. So I called in the crew.

CH: I thought most of your kind hung around further south?

RP: I don't know about that, I left them all long ago. But what you are failing to acknowledge is the level of inter-racial cohesion in the seabird community. We're not like you fucking idiot humans. When I refer to the crew, I refer to a number of different species, with whom I get along

172

marvellously. Anyway, I called them in and we formulated a plan. Obviously, first we had to ascertain where the plastic beer can thingy was most likely to be. It did not take us long to realise that we had no way of doing this.

CH: So what did you do?

RP: Well, when one cannot be certain, one makes an educated guess.

CH: Go on.

RP: We were aware of a small bay some way beyond the old golf course, where a lot of driftwood and the like accumulated on a regular basis. So it stood to reason that lots of things that got deposited in the sea could be found there. We resolved to direct the boat there, in the hope that it would mean that the two lovely boys found what they were looking for and had their consciences wiped spick and span.

—

Interview punctuated here with a surprised squawk and a thumping sound. A child starts to cry but the cry is muffled, as if in a different room, and things start to get fuzzier until the connection is lost completely.

It is a strange, pig-headed, competitive, pseudo-masculine, give-somebody-a-really-hard-handshake-to-show-that-you-mean-business, ultimately petty sort of hope that was driving Willard and Smoke to continue to look for this piece of water-borne plastic. Or that's what Smoke was thinking. It was his turn at the motor, and he was just holding it steady, directing them in a straight line, parallel with what they assumed to be the shoreline, although they could not see it.

Willard was stood right at the front, perfectly balanced, holding a pair of binoculars to his eyes and occasionally giving them both false hope.

The ridiculous thing was they had passed, and ignored, four pieces of litter in the sea as they went searching for their own. The only piece of litter that apparently mattered was theirs. They would clean up their own mess, and nothing more, it seemed.

Smoke was getting hungry. They'd been out at sea for what felt like the best part of the day now. It was certainly well into the afternoon. It wasn't that Smoke was bored. Sitting in that boat all day had been what they had always planned to do, so it didn't really matter that they were moving around whilst they did so. It was just that Smoke didn't really like having an objective, so to speak. He wanted to be free from any sort of ultimate goal, for the time being.

Smoke could tell that Willard was starting to lose interest as well. It was inevitable. Everything becomes boring after a while when you're fifteen. But Willard was stubborn. Willard had set them on this course, and Willard would pursue it until there was something – real or of his own imagination – that verified his giving up without it looking like he had failed.

Smoke started to worry that the engine would run out of petrol. He thought Willard would have probably been prepared for that, but he did not know for sure. Smoke often worried like this. He picked up his beer and took a sip, looking out at his friend. His friend did not look bothered. He did not look like he had forgotten to pack spare petrol. But he was rather preoccupied with the current plan, and so may just not be thinking about it. Smoke wondered if he should ask, but was concerned that doing so would make him look like a nag. Willard was his friend. He ought not to get ratty. But Smoke still did not want to ask. He started to look around the boat for a petrol canister, hoping that Willard would not notice.

Willard was coming towards him, stooping under the canopy and sitting down opposite Smoke.

"No luck?"

"No luck."

"Bummer."

"I'm starting to think that we might not find it."

"Did you bring spare petrol?"

"Yes, don't worry about that."

"I was just thinking that we might run out, was all."

"No, it'll be fine. To be honest I'm starting to think about packing it in, anyway."

"Right."

"It was only one thing. And it was an accident."

"Yeah. Still, though, sorry."

Willard moved and they both sat side by side with the motor between them. There was a slight breeze that shook the poles a little, but they were not worried about the canopy falling down. So instead it fell up.

It was snatched from above them, and dropped into the water a few metres behind them.

"Fuck."

"Why did that happen?"

"Let's go and get it."

They turned the boat around and went to fetch the canopy. When they reached it they dragged it on board but as it was now wet they couldn't put it back up without getting dripped on. They draped it over the front of the boat in the hope that the sun would dry it out. And then the heavens opened, but not with rain. With shit.

Runny white shit started to come down on them non-stop. Smoke looked up to see where it was coming from and got shit in his eye.

"Don't look up."

Willard obeyed and made a dive for the motor. The shit was falling from directly above them, and out in front there was what looked to be a shit-free zone. Willard thought something about the grass always being greener, but followed his instinct anyway and gunned the motor. They shot forward, but the shit shot forward too.

"Keep going. Try to outrun it."

Willard obeyed, but the origin of the shit seemed to change and now the gap in the shit-curtain was to their right. Willard steered the boat and they found themselves racing the shit-storm in an effort to outrun it. *Where was it coming from?* They both thought it but neither asked it. It was endless. It was accompanied by a beating sound but they daren't look up for fear of further shit-eye. They powered on, occasionally changing direction when the gap in the shit moved to one side. They put no thought into it. At one point the engine cut out and the boat stopped in its tracks, but so did the shit, continuing to fall on the stationary vessel. It was covered.

While the engine faltered Smoke stood up and peeled off his clothes, dumping them onto the white canopy. He stood there, whooping at the prow, not knowing what was going on, rapidly whitening until he looked like the Statue of David. Willard was laughing, equally baffled. He wasn't sure what he thought about seeing Smoke's dick. He supposed he didn't mind. Willard got the engine going again and the boat started moving and so did the shit.

This went on for about ten minutes, but it felt longer. It stopped as they realised that they were back towards the shore, with rocks either side of them. The water was getting shallower and Willard scraped shit from his eyelids and tried to make sure they didn't hit anything. Smoke said that he regretted taking his clothes off, but couldn't do anything about it now he was covered in shit. Willard said he didn't really mind. That it was a story to tell, if nothing else.

Smoke asked if the water was shallow and Willard said it was about neck deep. Smoke jumped in and started to scrub the shit off him. Willard didn't bother. He didn't think the water looked very inviting.

When Smoke was clean he climbed back into the boat and started to rinse his trousers in the sea. He then put the wet trousers on, commando, and sat down.

"The sea's filthy."

"What do you mean?"

"If you think what we did was bad, just look at the bottom of the sea here. The water's clear. Just look down at it. You may as well wash your face while you're at it."

Willard dunked his head under and blinked until his eyes could handle the salt and just about see. There was a shopping trolley and a punctured dingy weighed down by a rock. There were metal crates and carrier bags tangled in seaweed. He pulled his head out of the water and looked in the direction of the shore, about twenty metres down the narrow bay. Cans and bits of plastic floated atop browning scum, nuzzling the rocks and loitering in shallow rock pools created by the outgoing tide. The sand was littered with driftwood and more bags from long-defunct supermarkets. It was not a good beach.

"Smoke. What is going on?"

There was no point in asking. Smoke was as clueless as Willard. They both sat in the boat and looked at all the rubbish around them and underneath them. They looked up and in the distance a flock of birds was moving away from them. They didn't know where they were, but assumed they must be near the – or a – town in order for the trolley to be explained. That had to have been dumped.

They thought that they probably ought to do something, but it was outfacing. The sheer amount of rubbish – of wrongdoing – that surrounded them left them numb. They just looked at it, and then, unprompted, Willard started to nose the boat forward. He plucked one of the poles from a bracket at the back of the boat and started to sift through the rubbish.

"Maybe our thing is amongst all of this."

Smoke picked another pole and moved to the front of the boat. He sat down and started to poke through other bits of rubbish, as Willard steered them around the bay. Whenever something that was not theirs got caught on a pole, they shook it back into the water. They never found their beer rings.

After about an hour of looking they left the bay and managed to guess their way back home.

The Rainbow Big Band coupled with the Gay Oswaldtwistlians' Society of Hikers (G.O.S.H.)

Jenny had been given a lifeline after a few dry weeks. Acting on a tip-off texted to her from her armchair-bound father, she was once again heading towards the book shop, this time actually attending one of the many events advertised on the messily arranged noticeboards that littered the building's crowded wall space.

Her father illegitimately shared a room with his friend Connie at the home, got up to all sorts, and often talked about Connie's previous involvement with their local LGBTQ+ Big Band which, according to the pair of them, had been most eventful and a massive amount of fun. Naturally, as a product of their mutual desire to know everything that was going on in their community – and, once they had achieved that, everywhere linked to them in any way possible – they developed the habit of learning by heart the monthly social calendar for the group. In the process of learning the latest instalment of thrilling events lined up for Clitheroe's bisexual trumpet players, etc., they had happened upon an event taking place at Song Street Books. Her father – revealing an unexplained knowledge of his daughter's present interests – had been delighted. This emotion soon infected Connie and prompted the hastily written and terribly confusing text messages that were to send Jenny on her way to the event full of hope and carrying a fourth-hand, battered jaw harp found in Cash Converters as some sort of explanation.

The event was the annual literary meetup between the devoted Song Street regulars who were Clitheroe's Rainbow Big Band, and the Gay Oswaldtwistlians' Society of Hikers; an event set up by the leaders of both groups in an attempt to cultivate cohesion between the various LGBTQ+ societies and their allies spread throughout Lancashire. Graciously, according to the programme, the owners of Song Street Books, Song Street, Manchester, had been more than happy to host such an event in the city that was once an industrial behemoth within the clubs' fair county before it fucked off and started up a geopolitical side project of its own.

And the crux of the matter – the most exciting bit that had truly ignited the sensation of hope that burned inside her as she walked down Song Street – was the catering. Delicious local boutique fish and chip chefs Woodchips were to be providing all attendees with 'hearty scran'. Jenny did not really understand the burgeoning connection between this catering company and the bookish fellows involved in the filming of her advert, but she was certain that there was something in it. She felt she was on the brink of an idea with serious legs, but what would it lead to? Jenny wondered if she really was researching an article after all as she pushed open the shop's front door and made her way into a throng of chattering people holding books. She couldn't write a feature about a person without them knowing, surely? If she really was doing this for a piece then she would have to confront them one day. She didn't know if she would ever do that. She took out her jaw harp and tried to look like she was tuning it, or something. She was interrupted, in a friendly way.

"You a hiker or in the band?"

Jenny gestured with her instrument and smiled.

The man laughed.

"Wasn't aware that there was any of those in the Rainbow Big Band."

Jenny felt uneasy.

"Well, I'm here, aren't I?"

"Indeed. Anybody's welcome anyway. Any support is cherished."

"Thanks."

"You are?"

"Jen..." she didn't know why she did this: "... eva".

"Hi Geneva."

"You are?"

The man hesitated, like Jenny had done.

"Mick Krampman. And trust me, I'm about the most polyamorous person you ever will meet."

"Weird way to introduce yourself."

"We're more accepting than that here, usually."

"Sorry."

"You're welcome."

"..."

"If you have any questions just ask. I co-organised this occasion."

Jenny made her way across the entrance area in search of somebody else who looked like they knew what was going on but was not the man she had just spoken to. She did not like that man.

It was fairly easy to distinguish which of the people in the throng belonged to which organisation. As Jenny had suspected, the members of the big band carried their instruments, which complemented the large shoulder patches that adorned the tops of their uniform Levi's jackets. The hikers were the sort who wore walking boots, shorts and a fleece for every occasion, regardless of terrain and weather. Jenny felt that she would get on better with the big band lot and paraded her jaw harp like some form of identification in the hope that an absent-minded band member might notice and think they knew her, somehow.

Against the bookcase furthest away from the front door stood a fold-up table, upon which sat an enormous bowl of punch and a deep fat fryer, precariously left alone next to a stack of papers and shelves of books. The black book Jenny had become accustomed to checking for was there, but the people who owned it were not. Jenny peered into the deep fat fryer and watched the oil bubble, worried a little and then moved her body and her mind away from it. Nearby, two hikers were openly smoking what was just about the fattest joint Jenny had ever seen and upon seeing her they beckoned her over.

"You waiting for the food as well?"

Her mind was now back on the fryer.

"Should it be left alone like that?"

"We've been waiting too. Taking a while. They're over there – in the aprons – talking to the bloke who seems to own the place. They look like they're trying to be charming."

"I see them."

"We're just trying to stave off the hunger, if you fancy it?"

Jenny took a couple of hits and left them to it, walking towards the couple and the bespectacled man to whom the couple were talking. Ralph, she knew.

To avoid being noticed, Jenny slipped round the back of a nearby bookcase and walked along it to the point that she estimated was directly behind them. She was wrong and moved a few metres further along and got what she wanted. The nearest book to her was a how-to on something called 'Undercover Academia': something supposedly dreamed up by a certain Dr and Dr Perera whose names occupied the byline. It was slim and pale green. The spine was broken.

Jenny removed this book and a number of the ones that surrounded it, making a gap amongst the books large enough for her to insert her head and get closer to what it was that she wanted to hear. This position hurt her back, so she placed the books she had just removed onto the floor and used them as a parapet. She rested her head on the shelf.

"...interested in your new project."

"Well, thanks. We're excited about it too."

"Well in fact, we'd like to be involved if possible. If you look at our credentials, CV or whatever, there's really quite a lot of enticing stuff on there, I'd imagine."

"Certainly, experienced, well qualified."

"Thank you."

"I imagine that we are exactly the sort of people you can imagine forming a working relationship with, perhaps?"

"Certainly – well, depending on what it is that you have to offer."

"But you're open to suggestions, to... erm... things to be presented, to you?"

"Well sure. We need to link up with something to get this thing off the ground."

"Marvellous, and about this event, we really appreciate the partnership we've already founded through working together here."

"Of course, it seems to be a roaring success; one that would be impossible without the participation and ideas of the two esteemed groups who are meeting here today."

"Indeed..."

Jenny was interrupted by a tap on her shoulder. She turned round and found a man she recognised.

He had grown his hair out a little, and at a glance she deduced that the reason for this aesthetic manoeuvre was more to do with a lack of cash than it was style. Her gaze moved down his long nose and found a grin that was trying to be accommodating and managing to be slightly manic. His hand was still hanging, slightly above her shoulder. On his chest he wore a name badge; a blank space under the cramped, extra-small font spelling out the title of the event at which he was apparently working. He saw her gaze.

"We were supposed to write our names on ourselves. But I have messy handwriting so I couldn't' see the point."

"..."

"I think that I know why you are here again."

Jenny didn't answer immediately. She extracted her head from its uncomfortable position of trying to look over her shoulder whilst still inserted into the gap she had made in the bookshelf. Once out, she quickly stepped down from her stack of books for fear that her head would poke out over the top.

"You do?"

"I keep seeing you."

"You do."

"And it took me a while to twig, but I keep seeing them, too."

"Me too."

"You're on the advert. I saw you on TV only the other day. Like, the first time was a few weeks ago, max. And a few times since then. Pulling strings. Manipulating the media or whatever, maybe. And before that you were at my gig. Now you're here. Been here before, too."

"..."

Evidently Jenny had not been as inconspicuous as she had thought. Yes, she'd been here before, but what sort of shop worker remembers everybody? She must've stuck out. This was worrying.

"And they are always here. And they might have been at the gig too, I'm not sure. And now it turns out that they own that self-service chippy place that I went to and no doubt you went to."

"Go on."

She felt she needed to see what he was thinking on this subject.

"I knew I shouldn't have used my real name on the radio."

"..."

"Or in that fucking book."

"I know of the book."

"Journalists. You want to talk to me about that record cover, don't you? So do they."

"Sorry, what?" The young man seemed both so close and so far away from the truth.

"It was Ralph's mate Krampian's idea. It worked. He knows his marketing. Thing is, the record's immediate success didn't feel as good as I expected it to be. Hence the shyness that followed. I don't like being the centre of attention."

Jenny hadn't the foggiest idea what the man was talking about, but she decided to stay quiet in the hope that this accusation he was throwing both her way and in the direction of the pair she was investigating led somewhere exciting.

"But now everybody's all interested in what is apparently the birth of some sort of postmodern idea that the power of music is being conveyed through imagery, or some nonsensical bullshit like that, I think, but I'm not really sure."

"You're getting rambly."

"What?"

"Sorry, I'm a mumbler, carry on. You've... er... got me, it seems." Jenny had decided to go along with it.

"I wonder who is more in the know. You or them? You've both tracked me down this far, supposedly in the hope of an interview. I bet that's why those two are trying so hard to impress the boss over there. Some kind of attempt to get him to make me talk to them, perhaps. Maybe they think I have to do whatever Ralph tells me to..."

He was theorising to himself.

"Hang on," she interrupted him. "If you're so averse to journalists then why did you just come and start talking to me?"

He seemed a little stumped for a moment.

"Well, you've obviously tracked me down in every which way possible. May as well give you what you want so you leave me alone."

"Really, I don't really want anything."

"Bollocks."

Jenny wanted a way out of this one-way street.

"I reckon I've got what I want really. I'm more of a descriptive writer – I sort of paint a picture of a situation. I'll just describe my sighting of you and what you are up to and all that."

"Sounds weird and bad."

"It's... erm... it's what the readers want these days... I think."

"You sound good at your job."

"It's all about sizing up and eliminating the competition actually." Jenny's mind was working fast. "I'll have you know that I reckon that couple are in exactly the same game as me. And I know their sort, just from looking at them. They'll give out your address if they get it."

Ezra looked startled and Jenny felt slightly bad about exploiting what was proving to be his debilitating naïveté. She poked her head over the top of the bookcase and saw that the couple were behind their chip stand now, messing around with the deep fat fryer. She felt she might get more from her current companion.

"I have an idea. Let's go somewhere else. You can tell me what you think you have figured out about them so I can get a better idea of what they are up to. If I can get this story out about you – and believe me, I'll make it convoluted enough so that nobody can come and mob you – before any other

189

journalist then the rest will give up and move on to something else."

Ezra seemed to like the sound of that. And Jenny liked the sound of a story about a reclusive singer, hounded by incompetent but nevertheless amoral journalists with no respect for his privacy. Somebody would pay for that. Her dad would be into that sort of thing too. Maybe it was better than her original idea. She had already spoken to the subject as well.

Ezra moved round the side of the bookcase and made his way over to where Jenny could see Ralph was standing, next to the weird man who had greeted her upon entry. They were standing apart from the rest of the people, avoiding contact. He interrupted them and apparently excused himself, wordlessly, and then returned to Jenny and led her through a number of patterned rooms to a back door she was not aware of, and they emerged on a back street she didn't know about. This surprised her, as she had walked around the shop a few times the other week. She stood in the back street as Ezra gently let the door come to a rest in its frame without letting it make a noise. Maybe it was time to talk.

They walked down the street and Ezra told her that he did not have a car. Something to do with it being part of the puzzle that, once fully assembled, would awaken him to the terrific realisation that he was now totally reliant upon himself and would thus instigate some sort of internal crisis re: who he was and where he should actually be. It was confusing, but Jenny thought she got the idea and, despite herself, started to regret her teenaged ownership of a battered, fourth-or-maybe-more-hand VW hatchback, which at the time had been the vital ingredient for many an illicit beer run for less-mobile people she had wanted to sleep with. Youth. She thought about it. VW to ill-fated university attempt to boring job. Ezra: some sort of arts degree, no doubt, followed by potentially pretentious slumming it under the guise of musicianship and protesting that the retail work he was involved in was at least contributing to the network of knowledge and enlightenment. And a fuckload of paranoia. And a belief that car ownership actually meant anything, really. They were both lost, in her opinion.

Ezra began to divulge. Apparently the couple from the chippy had been all over the place of late. Coming into the shop. Talking to his boss, Ralph, about things that seemed totally unnecessary, pretentious and academic just so they had an excuse to be there. He had tried eavesdropping a few times. Nonsense about asking academic questions before and after people had eaten. Things to do with 'getting involved, gonzo-style with the subconsciously academic proletariat' – Ezra reckoned it made him feel sick. It was so transparent. There had to be an ulterior motive. Ezra had decided that the ulterior motive was him. He'd been keeping up with the fuss about the stupid album cover; he knew it was making him a desirable interviewee. Especially since

Ralph had credited the band with the artwork on the inner sleeve. And Ezra knew that Ralph did not care how he felt; Ralph loved the controversy around the artwork because people were talking about it. And when people were talking about it Ralph could tell people that somebody from the band was in some way associated with his shop. And this would no doubt indirectly attract people to Song Street. The couple of journalists were nearly as obvious as Jenny, he said, although they hadn't quite had the audacity to interrupt his viewing habits, as she had. What was the point in that anyway? All it did was make her more recognisable. As he spoke his voice quickened. He was winding himself up.

Jenny watched as Ezra made a last-minute gesture towards an intersecting passageway and headed down it without waiting for her. She missed the turning and had to spin round and turn the corner from the opposite direction. By the time she had done that Ezra was halfway up a fire escape, glancing over his shoulder as he ran. He tripped on a rusty step and fell hard onto the metal stairway. He looked at Jenny, his secretive escape clearly a failure.

"I thought this was the sort of thing people did straight after they tipped off a journalist."

"Yeah, works for me."

"You... erm... saw nothing. Okay?"

Jenny turned back around and left Ezra to ascend the staircase. She reckoned she was onto something due to the help of the paranoid shop assistant. He had been wrong about her, but his theory about the couple was something to go on. And even if false, it was a glamorous enough starting point from which to deviate, if necessary.

It took Jenny twenty minutes of wandering to get her bearings. Then she found a bus stop and got the next one home. On the way home she started to worry that if she'd been so recognisable to Ezra then surely the couple would also have noticed her shadowing them, especially if they were indeed the dogged journalists that Ezra thought they were.

Olwyn

I'm sitting in a GP's office trying to sort out this bloody gash across my left knee I got falling over on that fire escape. Not entirely pleased with myself over that whole debacle, but I'd heard about the event that was going on at work that day and, under the guidance of Angus, had smoked what he referred to as an 'emergency joint or two' before it started in an attempt to liven things up a bit. To be fair to us both, it sounded like it would be best enjoyed whilst attempting to be in some way psychedelic. Given the title, and all. Things unravelled, as they so often do when I try to experiment, and I developed extra-sensory abilities and all sorts of knowledge flooded into my brain from the ether that Angus always talks about and I don't believe in unless I'm drunk.

Doctors always have soft hands; they moisturise and must be forbidden from playing the guitar. What would a doctor write a song about anyway? The doctor moves her callous-free hands across my yellowing scab and I assume that she has never climbed through a broken window in order to have a look around a derelict building, or at least always remembers to wear thick safety gloves when she does so. I have tried to speak to the doctor, but she only answered me in writing and pointed to a post-it note that she had stuck to her forehead. It says that she is doing a sponsored silence and I wonder if she should really be carrying on in this fashion whilst working as a doctor. Then I realise that this must be why it was so easy for me to get an appointment despite having not been registered with a GP in this area since I left to go to university. They gave me the dud, it seems. Still, as long as I get fixed.

She reaches for a pen and writes a note asking why I didn't come to get this checked out a little earlier. I, having taken on board the habit of communicating non-verbally, shrug and smile. The smile comes across as a sort of grimace. She writes a note telling me that the cut is mildly infected and asks if I have been immunised from tetanus. I smile and nod, having recently phoned my mother to check this exact detail. I'm not totally impractical. This was a reasonably big step for me, too, as I don't like communicating with my parents as it makes me start to worry about what the fuck I'll do with them when they start to need looking after. And I'm poor and can't afford a home. And they've been fucked over by paying for my university and then by the teachers' pensions. And they're miserable because I never spawned grandchildren or provided them with anything to really boast about to their mates. Stuff like that. Out of pre-emptive guilt I try not to rely on them too much.

I reckon sponsored silences must be pretty hard to do successfully. Especially if the person doing it is a naturally talkative person. This doctor seems quite good at it, though.

It is because of this fear of never actually making

anybody proud of me – of never really living up to be much – that I have recently adopted a new strategy when visiting places that I expect will contain people of a more respectable standing than I. Places such as GP's offices, where the occupants, or at least a small portion of the occupants, will have high-class and useful degrees under their belts, soft hands and might or might not be attractive and have a lot of money coming their way over a period of time. Places where I feel that, if I look my most respectable and desirable, I may find an opportunity to progress in my life in a manner that ticks at least one of the boxes that correlate with the sort of things that constitute success when playing The Game of Life. The dry cleaner round the corner from the shop does this thing for me where, because I know him, if somebody doesn't claim their dry cleaning for a long period of time, and it fits me, I can take it. Thanks to this scheme, I have three reasonable suits cobbled together from leftovers. The reason they have been left behind seems to be because these articles of clothing were bought for one specific occasion, taken to be cleaned and forgotten about. The people who do this must have enough money to forget about things, so I never feel guilty about taking the clothes. Why they didn't hire them, I don't know. Nor do I know why they bother to clean them. Other leftover suits are the type where the cleaning just couldn't remove a stain. One example being a silvery stain on the inside of a pair of black suit trousers: evidently the product of a sly university ball hand job, or something like that. But the ones I take are always clean; just what you could perhaps call aesthetically questionable for certain occasions. But I cannot be fussy.

So I'm in this doctor's office with my white linen trouser leg rolled up and my salmon-pink linen jacket folded over the back of a spare chair on the other side of the room. My gold trim cravat itches so I always take that off after first impressions and shove it in my pocket. This time the doctor seems uninterested in me as a person, and there seems to be no place in this industry for somebody with my skill set. Nevertheless, having seen me, they might pass on my details to somebody else. I can always hope. A little extra to keep me going would never go amiss, really. There's fuck all coming from what I'm up to at the moment, really. Not enough for anything long term, even though, by some standards, I'm not entirely unsuccessful. Doesn't always feel that way, though.

Pushing On

It had been a bad day at the office. The police had been called because there'd been an assault outside the chip shop and a regular contributor to their black book – Thaddeus Wagstaff: badly behaved local schoolboy who had just broken another kid's jaw – had been taken away before he could fill in his answer for their latest question. They offered his victim – a friendly enough boy who maintained, through some sort of spontaneously invented sign language, that Thaddeus was his friend and that he harboured no ill feeling towards him – some free chips whilst he waited for somebody to give him a lift to A&E. He had declined on account of the fact that he would struggle to chew. They had planned for Thaddeus, as a sort of treat for his loyalty, to be the final entry in their book before they properly sat down with the data they had collected and started chasing up entries that stood out as potentially useful or interesting for further interview.

Now they had to settle for this irrelevant data analyst from Levenshulme who believed that saturated fats helped to temporarily cure his limp; something they immediately found to be untrue as the man staggered out of the door and, because one of his legs never properly relinquished its contact with the floor, tripped over the prostrate victim of Thaddeus' recent violent outburst. Funny, if it hadn't directly influenced them and their work and

198

also, as they realised in bed that night while mulling the occurrence over, made them feel really quite sad.

Before all that had happened however, they had been having something of a remarkably productive period; a series of days that brought them closer to this end point at a speed which they would never have been able to predict. Before that, things had been dragging along at a typical, academic pace. Lots of repetition; long-winded ruminations about the same things without making any decisions or even deviating in any sort of exciting way. The process had been dragged out in a way that was financially positive – what is academia if not paid procrastination; being rewarded with bits of metal and paper for delaying the moment when everybody realises that the answer that you have been idling towards is completely useless and not even that interesting? But it had been dragged out in a way that was, after a while, really quite boring. They were not prepared to endure that sort of thing, and neither was the guy who was throwing money at them. So things, ever so handily, picked up.

In the last week there had been more than sixteen pages of entries into the book. They attributed this to a local, community-minded busybody who had decided to throw a street party in the neighbourhood to celebrate something to do with the royal family. They had gone ahead and booked a fucking big band for it. A whole big band of big eaters. The cake stall got ignored and for the small price the couple were charging, along with the obligatory entry into their 'visitor's book' (which had been decorated with a crudely drawn image of a crown for the occasion), people flocked to clog their arteries and splutter on vinegar. Then they went back to fawning over newspaper clippings and commenting on the meaning of the aristocracy's various sartorial decisions.

Not that anything within those sixteen pages had been of particular note. It was more the sense of progression gained from filling blank pages with something. They had gained insights into people's opinions on gay rights before and after the heightening of their cholesterol levels. They had differentiated between the over and under fifties' trending points of view regarding the gentrification of Oxford Road, and then differentiated between the hungry and full-up subcategories within the two larger brackets. They had gauged on a scale of one to ten on how much of a fuckup the general concept of university in the modern age is in the minds of people before and after the consumption of a can of slightly warm Irn Bru. These were all things they did not need to know, as such, but they were certainly things that could contribute towards a lengthy footnote section, the presence of which in their planned work was mainly for the purpose of appearing more intelligent and well-researched than they actually were. It was one of those times where people think they have a good idea at the start, and then, midway through, when the initial buzz has worn off, they get bored and need something to bulk things out a bit.

Apparently, more than forty percent of people who eat chips more than twice a week, regardless of age, think that most elderly men look at least a *bit* like birds.

The same kid who first pointed out this similarity had loudly pronounced that chips were his second favourite food. He then said that his name was Keith. When asked by the woman what his top food was he replied with the brand name of the food the woman also considered to be her favourite. This prompted a conversation about the viability of a breakfast cereal being somebody's favourite food; something both the boy and the woman were extremely passionate about. The boy said that the advert had scared him, though.

Wandering Eye

As they came to the edge of the shadow of the big wheel, they parted. And Jenny had to decide which one to follow throughout this temporary separation. She moved leftwards and found herself following the woman, who was running her hands against the fence as she walked by, occasionally leaning inwards and placing all her weight on the thin metal poles. As she walked, the woman reached up and tried to run her hand along the pole that ran across the top of the fence. She did all of this quickly, absentmindedly, not even breaking her stride. Jenny knew how the woman must feel. She was herself a fiddler, pulling leaves from trees as she walked past, kicking loose gravel on the pavement, things like that.

As the woman reached up to touch the top of the fence Jenny realised that she had never seen her bare arms. They had always been clad in long-sleeved shirts, sheepskin coats, Burberry scarves, other intellectual-looking things. Today the woman wore a loose-fitting long-sleeved granddad shirt. When the woman reached up and touched the pole that ran across the top of the fence the sleeve fell down to her elbow. By now Jenny had caught up with the woman and realised that she was risking being noticed, but she was drawn to what she could see. Across the woman's forearm was a network of sadness, each link at its own personal point in the healing process. Jenny checked herself and slowed down, dropping back a few feet until the image was in her mind rather than in her sight. The woman was now beyond the perimeter of the big wheel and was rejoining her husband. Jenny followed her path exactly, a few seconds delayed.

DIY

One of those unnecessary cereal cafes that people only go to in order to take photographs. People on law vacation schemes come here, having suggested something as devilish as a 'quirky brunch' to their freshly acquired friends/colleagues/rivals/enemies/all-of-the-above, and try and pretend they are finding the whole thing fun. But one of them is worried that their shirt is blatantly unironed and somebody's shoes are hurting but they are locked in an unspoken competition with the other person whose shoes are also evidently hurting and cannot be the first to swap to flats. And the man behind the counter looks beardy-hungover-chic until you realise his late night takeaway curry keeps making him fart and whenever you go up to order another bowl of overpriced cereal you can't help but breathe in his airborne microshits.

Jenny never thought these places would spread this far north but they had done. She thought they'd try to spread and hit a wall made out of something like grey-suited Northampton residents trying something new on the weekend and deciding, almost immediately, that they'd stick to what they knew. Then, tails between legs, the peddlers of the type of all-day breakfast that you eat exclusively with a spoon would go back to London. Or so she had naïvely hoped.

Jenny thought all of this as she stared into a bowl

of something named Austerity Crunch – a cereal that tried to make a political statement out of the fact that the company was skimpy on the number of ingredients they were willing to bother with – and whirled her spoon through the somehow-wetter-than-usual milk. At one of the tables outside of the main cafe, and barely in view due to the depressing busyness of the place, sat the couple Jenny was actually starting to get quite bored of. They were next to a stand filled with copies of smug music magazines from London. They each had a copy, but neither of them was reading. She reckoned that her notebook had not actually left her pocket for a couple of days. Nothing even vaguely exciting had taken place. She was done with all the minutiae. Certainly, they were an interesting pair, but not exactly the sort you could use as inspiration for a piece of writing that would prove to be the pivotal point in your life. Jenny was increasingly unimpressed. Her interest now lay with the paranoid shop assistant, really. Still, she persisted.

She watched the couple out of the corner of her eye and continued to stir her cereal, which was growing soggy and starting to disintegrate.

The woman had bought an entire box of whatever it was she was eating. Evidently earning nicely, then. She poured some of the cereal into the bowl and an orange packet fell out and caused the milk – which was brownish, suggesting that it was about to be used for at least the second time – to splash over her scarf. She wiped her scarf down and looked pleased to pick up the orange packet and put it into her pocket, without even looking at it. The man was watching her warily, as if the free gift was something of a big deal to him. But it could've just been because he was realising that his wife still got excited about free gifts from cereal packets.

Across from her there was a grown man eating chocolate cereal with bits of Kit Kat in it from out of half of a fucking Easter egg. But the egg was starting to melt and he was becoming visibly panicked, as he stuffed the food into his mouth in his own unnecessary race against time. An aggressive flirtation with gluttony.

Jenny decided to tune into a few of the conversations that were going on around her.

"This is so cool. Like, who'd have thought it!? It's, like, chocoception, or some shit like that."

The sort of person who actually spoke as if their sentences ended with both an exclamation mark and a question mark.

"You see, and don't tell people about this, but I have two phones. And I put one on vibrate and, since Lindsay left me, I put it up my arse and ring it all the time. Thing is, yesterday, when I rang it, Lindsay answered. And now I think we might be back together."

"I consider myself a progressive, community-minded conservative."

That one had dribbled milk down his front.

"I've just started to really get off on the idea that Nabokov might actually have been the first, like, the first anarchist."

"You should read Ayn Rand."

"This place is revolutionary."

"Rasputin. That's where I'm at. Logistically, anyway."

"Hey, mix that chocolate one over there with the leftover ketchup from this Maccies. I *dare* you."

"I don't care."

"Let's try out that new coffee place across the road after this."

The phrase: 'culture vulture'.

Jenny looked out of the window and saw that the couple had left. She got up and didn't bother paying her bill.

Owzthat?

So it is kind of handy that, after a couple of weeks, something interesting finally goes and happens.

Jenny is back at Woodchips – was it supposed to be some sort of highbrow pun or something that she just didn't get? – and now almost positive that they at least know her face as a regular diner, if nothing more. Better be careful. But she can't resist: leaning against the counter eating curry-half-chips-half-rice and staring out of the window, ears tuned in to a high-pitched, squat lady wearing a charity T-shirt and telling them that they should come along to some sort of meeting or church or something that she regularly attends. The squat lady actually describes it as 'supreme'. Her voice cuts over the general hubbub easily; it's as if Jenny's listening accidentally.

The couple ask the squat lady to write the name and address of the place in their book and then tell her yes, they'd be there and Jenny supposes that that's her weekend planned then. One last try at this. Not exactly what Ezra had suggested they might be up to, but some sort of dubious religious conversion, and its impact upon their pursuit of the ever-elusive artist, could be something worth mocking in order to engage a few people. If it doesn't pan out like that then Jenny is resigned to the idea that she might have to start heavily fictionalising; trusting her own imagination in a way that she does not yet feel completely ready to do. But money is getting tight as she has been repeatedly rejecting other work in the hope that, by devoting more time to this new idea of hers, she will be more likely to stumble across something that will ensure its eventual success.

Sunday morning comes around slowly, separated from the moment in the chip shop by cavernous, unemployed time. Boredom has that knack of making everything seem pointless. Every opportunity to fill one's time seems an unlikely, fool's pursuit. Jenny is lying on her bed when she realises it is finally time to go, and she cannot remember when she last did something properly memorable. She figured that she must be doing this all wrong quite a while ago, now.

The most recent recognisable landmark was Manchester's John Rylands Library, and that was twenty minutes ago. Twenty minutes of total zone-out, though, so maybe something had cropped up since then but it had just gone unnoticed by Jenny, who walks, headphones in, permanent scowl, perennially fucked off, probably to the south, but she always gets disorientated with regard to the points of a compass as soon as she is surrounded by tall buildings. Almost intentionally so. It's part of the magic of the place, some would perhaps say. Jenny notices and largely ignores the significant presence of homeless people. Perhaps a twinge of guilt – a desire to, if she had spare money herself, do something to help. Buy a second house and let people live in it for free or something. Something grand and unrealistic like that. She is, she reckons, only about five minutes away from her destination.

She turns three more corners in total. Between each one there is a stretch of narrowish road. It has been quite a long walk in the end. The building she wants is obvious because of the throng of people milling about outside looking happy. It is, Jenny thinks, the sort of building in which people's lives change. Not because it gives off the aura of somewhere particularly spiritual or anything. Just that outside, attached to the gate under which people walk to enter the building's grounds, there is a banner that says 'prepare for your life to be changed'. A major promise to make to people who come in week in, week out. Are their lives changed every week? Anyway, Jenny looks at the banner and thinks that people are more likely to leave under the impression that their lives have been changed if they enter the building believing that this is undoubtedly what is going to happen.

Before Jenny gets to the end of the road – the building sits in a cul-de-sac – the throng of people hurry through the gate and the industrial doors that were being held open by two youngish boys. Jenny gets to the gate and walks under it, stopping briefly to read the noticeboard pinned to a tree just on the other side of the threshold. It takes only a moment to ascertain that this meeting place is certainly not used by any of the more established religious groups. Tuesday mornings offer a class in how to read the future from the dregs of cereal and milk at the bottom of your breakfast bowl. Thursday afternoons host spiritual-face-painting sessions to the accompaniment of the first ten seconds of a number of Pink Floyd songs, all listed in a footnote at the bottom of the poster. Apparently deciduous plants are strictly forbidden in all places of worship, *especially* within forty seconds' walk of the crèche facilities. If you want, you can open up a tab at the tuck shop, but you have to open it up under a pseudonym that humorously puns on the name of a retired football player. Jenny prepares Frank Werther's-ton – not great, but adequate – and sets off towards the industrial doors, now firmly closed, wondering whereabouts the couple will be, and what they must be making of all of this.

The doors open in a way that Jenny would tentatively call languidly. And silently. Jenny cannot hear anything inside the cavernous warehouse. The few skylights, way above her, have had their glass replaced with the stained variety. There is a gantry running around the edge of the room, unoccupied, and through the gap between the platform and the waist-high railing that runs along it Jenny can see that it is lavishly carpeted. The congregation of people in the room do not seem to notice – or at least do not care – that they have a latecomer amongst them, and Jenny slides into a cushioned chair right at the back of the building, next to a metal, spiral staircase. She cranes her neck, her ears gradually registering that the room is not in fact practically silent, but rather, fading in and out of speakers dotted throughout it in a sequence that leads the listener to believe that the sound is circumnavigating the space, there is a dull humming noise. Upon closer inspection Jenny notices that the head of each individual member of the congregation is rotating, ever so slightly, in accordance with the illusion of the sound's circumnavigation, with respect to where each person is sat. Jenny notices the tuck shop, and sees that its wares are limited and seem only to cater for those eating in the early mornings.

There does not appear to be anybody in charge. Jenny looks around, hoping to spot the couple, or at least the squat woman who invited them to this place. Instead she finds herself staring at an object that is in the middle of the group of people, who are actually sitting in a tight circle. All of them are facing the same direction – away from her – so that rather than being the centre of attention, this object that Jenny has just noticed is instead sort of just sat amongst the group of people and largely ignored. The object is a video cassette player, not plugged in to anything, just sat there. It is plastic and looks to have been made quite recently – valueless – making its presence all the more confusing.

A man stands up. He is wearing striped blue-

and-white pyjamas, like a teddy bear she remembers seeing on a computer game years ago, and Jenny assumes that this is the leader. She cannot see his face very well because he is blindfolded, much like she was in her advert. Only his mouth, chin and hairline are unobstructed by a thick strip of fabric that matches the pyjamas. He blatantly has an erection, which Jenny feels is entirely inappropriate, but perhaps he has been watching yoghurt adverts. In his hands is a comically large spoon, which he holds out in front of him, and begins to move in a stirring motion. In time with his quickening stirring of the giant spoon the congregation's heads rotate, also gradually increasing in speed, and Jenny notices that the humming noise seems to be circumnavigating the room at a faster pace, too. It is, if nothing else, well, well rehearsed. But Jenny starts to worry that it might – ineffably – be something more than that.

Jenny decides to get a better look at the situation. She slips out of the chair and moves, sidestepping carefully onto the first step of the spiral staircase. Nobody turns. She climbs the staircase slowly, and begins to make her way, hobbling in a crouch, along the gantry that runs down the right hand side of the room, advancing towards the group until she is just behind the people closest to the back. She peers out of the gap between the gantry platform and the rail, her head protruding over the enormous space. Directly below her is a speaker, and she notices that the humming coming out of it is getting quieter.

After a few seconds it fades almost completely and the spoon man's voice – she can tell it's him from the exaggerated movement of his mouth as he speaks – comes out of the speakers over the top of the now barely audible humming. His arms are still moving, as are the heads of those in the room. Jenny realises that she is subconsciously rotating her protruding head and stops this immediately. The man is talking about everybody being welcome, and then tells everybody to stay relaxed, as this is the only way that they can communicate with the person whose very existence has only recently become a matter of great importance to them; a realisation born of some sort of sudden *awakening*. He points the spoon directly towards the general area inhabited by the video cassette player and then resumes his stirring. He then begins the process of spinning some lengthy, elaborate bullshit about a person who can control time like one seemingly controls time with the play, pause, rewind and fast-forward functions on a video cassette player, and any sort of spell that the place had somehow established over Jenny is immediately broken. This is fucking ridiculous. The man once again somehow points his spoon directly at the general area occupied by the video cassette player and then resumes his stirring and tells the people in the room to all stay perfectly focused, as the only way that they can summon this person who can control reality like it is being played on a video player is through the magnetism of their communal longing. The people in the room are making noise for the first time, and the noise is a murmur; unanimous agreement with whatever it is the man is going on about. The people in the room have completely bought it – Jenny makes the assumption that they bought it a long time ago. Jenny wonders how long this has been going on. She looks again for the couple and realises that, unless they are hiding like she is, they are not there. As far as she can tell, neither is the squat woman who was in the charity T-shirt. Jenny, paranoia now fully setting in, starts to worry that the couple have indeed noticed her, and that this is some sort of elaborate prank to freak her out, or get her into some kind of mess, purely just to finally get rid of her. The man now lifts up his spoon and carves a downward parabola into the air in front of him. Jenny feels trapped. She feels pointless and useless. She feels like she has no future whatsoever, especially if she carries on with this stupid, self-appointed quest. Why on earth did she ever believe that she could do this? What was the point? Her eyes follow the curve as she feels all of this pass through her mind and she becomes tempted to just roll off the balcony, just to feel a fall she inexplicably is now sure would follow a similar trajectory to that of the spoon's graceful movement.

Then something entirely strange happens. As Jenny allows her head to droop further and further below the level of the gantry, still unnoticed, at least in a physical sense, by those beneath her, she catches blurry, sleepy sight of something. What she sees forces her, out of outright fear for her own belief in reality, to shake off the effect of this place; an effect that she had until so recently been certain she was naturally immunised against thanks to her inherent northern cynicism. In front of her eyes, unfocused as they now are, floats – or perhaps it is mounted against the far wall – a framed still of Jenny, mid-shock-fall, blindfolded, hair buoyed by the rushing air, the edge of a cherry picker's cage just visible beneath her feet. Well, what the fuck's that about? Jenny shimmies herself backwards and onto the gantry. She sits upright and shakes her head, making herself ready to crawl back along the balcony. The service appears to have ended anyway, and Jenny hopes to leave by merging with those also exiting the building. Slightly fearful that this is the sort of place where everybody knows everybody, she resolves to keep her head bowed. Down the spiral stairs, towards the languid doors, quickly. Only looking up she realises that people aren't leaving. They are queuing up at the tuck shop, a few metres to the left of the main entrance. Jenny glances that way and maintains her swift pace. At the door a man smiles and she realises that it is the man who is the most polyamorous person she will ever meet. This does it for Jenny and she is out of the door and down the road, somehow clutching a leaflet that she supposes the most polyamorous man she will ever meet thrust into her hand.

<u>And what path, would that be?</u>

"Let the follower... like... become the followed."

Ralph exhaled and leaned back, knocking a book from the shelf behind his head. He passed a joint to me and I declined. Paranoia was something I had enough of already. He opened a polystyrene box and took out one of those fancy burgers that have little flags in the top buns and just absolutely devoured it in about three bites. I didn't even see him take the flag out. I had been telling him about my issues with the journalists and trying to get him to take some of the blame for being part of the contingent that insisted on that specific piece of artwork.

"Aren't you going to ask about my leg, by the way? That injury I told you about? The last time I did some of Angus' shit. And here I am, doing it again, thanks to your passive smoke."

"That? That was weeks ago."

"No it wasn't. It was, like, a few days ago."

"No mate, it was weeks ago. You took a day off for it, for some daft reason. Look in the log book."

I went over to Ralph's desk – a miniature ironing board stood up on its fifteen-centimetre legs towards the back of the tent – and picked up the only item on it. Ralph was right. It had been weeks ago. This was worrying. My life was slipping away from me.

"It was two and a half weeks ago."

"Yep, told you."

Ralph was looking at me a bit funny and I assumed I was showing my instability.

"What's up with you, Ezra?"

"Well I told you about that woman who is following me."

"Wait, what?"

"You know, the one in that advert we saw."

Ralph seemed to suddenly have total recollection, as if he always knew what I was on about. Although maybe I was just being paranoid. He nodded in enthusiastic understanding.

"Well, I spoke to her, she's not the problem. There's this other thing I haven't been telling you about."

"Hmmm?"

"There's some others. More journalists, I reckon. More people because of the bloody art. I don't get the interest. It's messing me about, man."

"Stick it out, man, it'll mean your record sells and you can finally stop working here, if you want."

"Seriously Ralph, I hate it. I think I'm doing a story with one of them. We chatted about it. They say that then they'll just leave me alone."

Ralph allowed himself a wry smile.

"Journo bullshit, Ezra, mate. Once they've got their hooks in you they're there for good, I reckon."

"I just keep seeing them everywhere. They've been here. Two of them. The two I'm worried about. They've been here a few times."

"Really? What'd they look like?"

"They look clever, like. A bit tweedy. Floppy haircuts. Glasses. They're South Asian. A few weeks ago they were selling fucking chips. You must know who I'm talking about. I mean, talk about weird disguises. But they're good. They don't even act like they're watching me. They just get close – at the same events, in the same room, talking to people I know. They're worming their way towards me."

By now Ralph looked to be getting rather baked. His face twitched a little as he imagined the people I was describing to him, trying, or pretending to try, to remember who they were.

"You say it's making you paranoid. Is this paranoia debilitating? Does it bug you a lot, sort of, does it unsettle you and stuff?"

"Well, yeah."

"Lots of different people following you is bound to do that, I guess."

"Well, yeah."

"Don't know who is watching when, and all that kind of thing."

"Well, yeah."

"Ezra, you're on loop, vary up your fucking vocabulary, man."

"Sorry. But you're on the right lines with what you are saying."

"Cool. Well then listen to what I said earlier. Ages ago, today. You remember?"

I wracked my brains. I thought I could just about remember. Ralph told me anyway.

"Freak them out. Scare them off. You can do it, Ezra. You'll find it easy, probably."

He mashed the remains of the joint against the miniature ironing board and left a dark brown stain on the cover. The stain glowed orange around the hole in its centre. The air in the tent was fuggy but Ralph shook his head when I made a movement towards opening the door flap. It was nighttime.

"Don't open the door at night, Ezra."

And so we both lay down amongst the fug and slept until the morning. When I woke up Ralph was gone and there were some loose, synthetic hairs on the floor of the tent and they were wrapped around one of those stupid little burger flags.

A Distinct Lack

For the last week or so Jenny had been drifting, no longer all that invested in her mission thanks to that one bad experience. She thought that she'd got the message. That this couple, journalists or cult members or pranksters or just chip shop owners or whatever they were, were not happy about being followed around.

Naturally, she began to make regular moves pubwards, usually armed with a book and/or a willingness to talk to anybody who happened to be there. She recontacted a few close friends and arranged to meet up with them in evenings for more civilised attempts at socialising and filling her time. She even wrote to her old editors and told them she was available for work in the hope that she could make a bit of money. She knew she was reasonably good at that, at least. She hadn't told her dad about the whole crazy scenario yet, but she thought he'd be disappointed and thrilled in equal measure, and then suggest some sort of ambitious artistic endeavour regarding the church, which Jenny would refuse to even consider because was she fuck ever going back near that bastard place. She didn't want to make sense of it. She didn't even want to try and see if that was all possible. Real or not, it had happened as far as she was concerned.

So naturally, it was unwelcome when aspects of her recent past started to creep up on her. She had decided to spend a night out on a reunion with some of her friends from her vague association with the M.W.W.W.W. (Manchester Women Who Want War – a collective made up of people who enjoyed wartime throwback exhibitions). This was an enjoyable occasion, with the only negative being that the couple were once again, somehow, present. And they seemed as surprised about that as she was.

She was stood at the bar, talking to the group's leader, Theresa, who had, once, sat across from a semi-inebriated but lucid Jenny in a different bar. Although Jenny hadn't known her then. During a period when Jenny's attendance with the group had plummeted in its frequency to pretty-much-never, Theresa had taken over as leader and her predecessor, Agnes, relinquished all responsibility completely and found herself in a dementia home. Upon rejoining the group, Jenny had recognised her new leader immediately – although a little hazily, and had set out to ask whether the recognition was reciprocated. Theresa – who at that point had introduced herself to Jenny only as Ms Stern for the sake of formality – answered in the negative and they'd struck up some kind of loose friendship ever since.

As they finally got served by a barman with some sort of dreadful wallpaper pattern scrawled permanently all over his arms and hands, the small section of unoccupied bar next to them had been filled by none other than the bloody couple Jenny had

actively been avoiding. They ordered their drinks –
all four of them – simultaneously, and the barman,
who was struggling under the sheer complexity
of the seven-drink order he had just taken from
numerous parties, kindly gave them enough time to
wait for awkward small talk to become a necessity.
The couple turned to speak, betrayed their almost-
immediate recognition of one or the other of the
women they now faced and caused both Jenny and
Theresa to scarper, in opposite directions, to the
bathrooms.

Here's the Head Or Tail of it

They sat there, on the settee, chewing, swallowing, watching, still watching, chewing another mouthful, swallowing, noticing a stain on the carpet, deciding that the other was in a funny mood that day.

They had seen it for the first time about a week beforehand. As time went on it was appearing with what felt like increasing frequency. At first it would come up intermittently – perhaps every other ad-break or something. Then, after a few days of that, it would come up in every ad-break and they'd started to get a bit annoyed with it. So they'd stopped watching TV for a couple of days, only then, when they restarted, it was there again, happening more frequently if anything. And even the adverts that weren't that exact one were in some way, all of a sudden, related. Everything they saw on television would force them to recall the specific advert with clever allusions and intertextuality and all that sort of thing. It was subtle; impressively so. But that didn't necessarily make it good in their minds. And besides, they already bought the product in vast quantities at the woman's behest. So this cartel-type programming arrangement wasn't going to do anything to affect their lives.

The man got up out of the settee and walked over to the television, bending stiffly forward to switch it off at the mains. The woman said that she thought it was a good advert – that it stuck with you – however it was dangerously close to becoming a constant presence, thus losing its shock value and assimilating with all of the other things that take place every day, frequently, and go totally unnoticed. The woman pointed out, with near-comical graveness when one considers the subject matter at hand, that it is very easy to unnotice things.

"But don't you think it's a bad thing for a woman jumping off a building to be assimilated with all the other unnoticeable, commonplace things, like the fridge buzz?"

"It's just an advert."

"I don't like it. It means that that's become an ordinary thing to happen."

"It hasn't. But it might."

They discussed the potential of something like that becoming normal. If something like that became normal, could it be possible that people would start reacting in that way in situations that really didn't – or, at least, previously often wouldn't – rationalise it?

Then the man said that this was the problem with the sort of thing they always did. That all of this pondering – some might call it overthinking – never actually applied to anybody.

But hopefully not this time, the woman pointed out. What they were doing with the chip shop was helpful. They were engaging directly with people, and they were supplying a service, and what they were asking was varied and covered a large demographic. In a moment of out-of-character positivity, the woman went so far as to say that they could have hope in what they were doing now. It was a banker, she said. They had basically been commissioned – and by somebody with a significant degree of power, no less. Somebody who had hinted at connections.

The man was so brave as to pose a few what-ifs; each was swiftly rebuked. This was something the woman was willing to believe in. And if not, well then, yes, drastic action would have to be taken. And then the man said that it never hurts to be prepared.

This suggestion of the necessity of being well prepared sent the woman on a downward spiral of paranoia; worrying that things about which she had previously been certain – little, organisational details that would be important over the next few days, weeks – were in some way incorrect, and she walked over to the telephone mounted on the wall in the kitchen and dialled a number. The number got her speaking to their benefactor who, much to the woman's relief, confirmed that their deadline was indeed at the time she had been sure that it was, and told them to take their time; that there was no rush as long as they didn't keep him waiting in such a way that he became aware that he was, in fact, waiting.

Meanwhile, the man was inspecting what appeared to be yet another grease stain – the bastards were appearing as if he'd taken out a subscription: something he had not considered when the pair of them had settled upon the service they would be providing as a front for their research. He reached over to the side table next to his seat and picked up a paperback, opened it at the dog-eared page and started to take in what was written down. He was unconvinced. He placed it back down on the table, almost in the exact same place as that from which he had first moved it, and looked at the blank television screen. Minutes passed as he gazed into it. He saw the woman, blindfolded, agape, then saved. Feet back on something solid. Crisp rain.

Forty minutes later and they were amongst the streets of central Manchester, under the drizzle, walking down a slight slope towards Exchange Square. They intended to turn right once they escaped the hubbub of shitty buskers and laden carriers lugging things they didn't need in the direction of the nearest bus stop. Blink and you'll miss it, but the man accidentally kicks a pebble and it smacks a Hare Krishna bloke right in his isolated ponytail and that's the reason the man ducked out of view, behind his wife, sheepishly laughing, as the enlightened one slumped forward on his mat, howling.

Another mile or so in the direction that people generally don't travel and they walked through the front door of a store claiming to be an 'ocular specialist' – not part of the original plan, which had been to stick outside and get some fresh air – and shortly afterwards, re-emerged into the great outdoors having purchased a pair of binoculars.

<u>Final vieW: found.</u>

And Jenny was starting to feel some element of pain, as she pressed it further into her eye sockets, trying to figure out why this sort of thing would ever be considered worth looking at – wondering if she was missing something – trying to utilise some intellectual power she knew that she didn't have to recall, from somewhere, some book or something, the relevance of an image of an envelope sliding down the inside of a door, doormatwards, the letterbox somehow caught midway through slamming shut, spring-loaded, the whole time aware, somehow, that this was important to someone.

Jogging through the Dead Head

Ralph suggested straight-up engagement; to face them off in such an aggressive manner that they leave me alone. I have elected to run away. I have decided to do this in two different ways.

Running away method one: I have decided to run away mentally – I will make myself as uninteresting as possible, in an effort to get them to move on to something else. I will become the most mundane man alive.

Method two: I am literally *on the run*. Or, well, a run.

Legs pumping; arms moving in a way I hope doesn't look too silly; coughing up phlegm; not for a moment finding it meditative but instead spending every second thinking about the moment I can stop running. I have taken up jogging. I feel that method two supports method one absolutely.

I am embarrassed to be seen running. I have bought a pair of shorts. I accidentally bought those really short ones that only ever seem to be worn by men with receding hairlines and concrete jaws. *I am a man. Look at my fucking mega-thighs. I am forty-seven and I can still run up a hill faster than you can achieve orgasm or figure out how to turn the shower down to a tolerable temperature.*

I have borrowed a friend's Edinburgh half-marathon finisher's shirt. I hope it makes other, more proficient runners think that, although I may be a bit out of shape now, I was once like them. I was once able to run for a long time and not feel despair.

I have bought some running shoes. They make me look like a twat. I can't figure out what kind of socks I am supposed to wear with them.

I'm running now, actually. Or, well, staggering along a canal, in the wintery light, having checked that none of my friends are going out for a hungover brunch or anything for fear that, if they were, they might spot me. I am passing buildings which are, as you might expect, completely, blissfully stationary. Jogging makes me have these thoughts.

I wish I was a building, then I wouldn't have to be running.

I wish I was dead.

That one is another one that seems to crop up regularly. People say that so much. I say that so much. I never mean it and very rarely does anybody else who says it. Maybe we should pay more attention to the ones who never say it.

I come across a few geese and, as I gain on them step by step, I realise that they are not going to move. This induces panic, naturally. The geese own the canal. I am an intruder, and I am scared. They remain stationary – *I wish I was a stationary goose, then I wouldn't have to be running* – and I start to assess my surroundings so that I might figure out a route by which I can bypass them. There is none. I must forge through the hostile feathery barrier and hope that my twattish trainers and the knobbly, inappropriately besocked ankles that sprout from within them, go unpecked.

My mind is totally engaged by the goose problem. It occurs to me that I am not bored and the situation in which I find myself is not boring. I speed up in the hope that, should anybody be following me, they might not want to put in the effort to keep up.

The geese notice my graceless acceleration and they are not happy. One of them makes that caustic hissing noise that I think what they do when they feel like they have a dickhead on their hands (wings? feet?) and need to act, whether they like it or not. I realise this is the most threatened I've ever felt.

Goose thoughts right now: *I wish he wasn't running. Then he wouldn't be here and we wouldn't have to deal with him.* Even the geese – my adversaries – agree that running is not the best thing I could be doing at this time.

Three geese start to move towards me. I do not know if this is natural behaviour for geese – to run head on into a high speed threat. I begin to worry that this is testament to my own self-delusion with regards to how fast I actually manage to run. I mean, I am not claiming to be hurtling around the M4 postcode area at any kind of particularly impressive speed, but I would've hoped I was at least fast enough to intimidate a two-and-a-bit foot high waterfowl. If that is how tall geese are. You get the idea. So on top of genuine fear, my confidence had taken yet another knock. A knock inflicted by a goose – an animal absolutely incapable of knocking. Think about it – imagine a goose hits its beak against a door. It is not a knock. It is at best going to sound like a tap.

I think I am going to give up smoking. Or at least move on to one of those electronic screwdriver things you can smoke inside. I will take the eternal hit in terms of image, I think. Phlegm comes up involuntarily from my tarred innards and, contrary to the very thing I want most at this exact point in time – to placate the geese – hits the lead goose in the face. Oh bollocks. I actually say sorry and slow down.

Speed up, speed up. Fuck. You fucking plonker. Run. Jump. Super Mario. Where are the mushrooms, the coins, the *fun*?

One goose phlegmed, two geese hurdled. The rest are in my wake. I have won. I feel so *fit*. Never mind the Edinburgh Half Marathon. What about the nylon T-shirt, which would set you back sixteen quid, to commemorate the auspicious occasion when I evaded three vicious geese using nothing but my guile and pace? I am going to get one made.

I go under a bridge and on the other side of the water there are two blokes shitting into a laundry basket. I can't figure out how they got there. They smile at me and shout 'run Forrest run' and carry on shitting. *I wish I was shitting in a laundry basket. Then I would be stationary and I wouldn't be running.*

Back out in the open air. It is a cool morning. I have to decide where I want to go next. I leave the towpath and decide to venture slightly out of the city. I forget that I am going to have to make my way home at some point and make headway in the most inconvenient direction.

The good thing about running in Manchester is that it is largely flat. I do not know what I would do if I had to overcome slopes of even the slightest gradient. I know I am weak-willed. Some might say pathetic. No doubt the short shorts men would laugh at my pallid, wobbly thighs. *I am a man and however vigorously I move, my body stays completely still. There is no wobbly flesh at all. Even if I had double Ds they would remain stoic in a gale. And I wouldn't be wearing a sports bra. Watch me run up this hill. I wish my wife still loved me.*

I feel like running is often the product of some sort of insecurity. Especially with the ones who say they run because it gives them time to think. The 'I just need a bit of head space, man' types. Bullshit. I can absolutely guarantee that these people really just want a break from the washing up, feel guilty about how much time they devote to their own penis, or wish they were somebody else. Running allows you to pretend that you are somebody else. You pass people at a faster pace than usual. They get a shorter time in which to judge you. You hope this means they gloss over a few of your otherwise obvious flaws. Maybe they get a fleeting glance and imagine something above and beyond what you actually are. It is funny how often people equate good health to morality. The demonisation of smokers is a great example. People often assume smokers are bad people. People often look at somebody smoking and think less of them. People judge other people who only eat frozen food. Other people automatically assume the fat are also lazy. Now that I run, I feel better about myself. But why? It is a fallacy. I am helping nobody else through running. My trainers were made in Vietnam, probably by children. Probably by starving children. But I run in these shoes, so I am good.

Does any of this make sense? *If I was stationary, I could think with greater clarity. I wouldn't be coming out with this irrational pseudo-philosophy. I could sit in an armchair and ponder and reach rational conclusions. But because I am running my thoughts are constantly interrupted by the thought: 'I wish I was dead'. Maybe this is the 'clarity' that people think they reach while running. Maybe it is all a delusion. But now I have realised that, have I indeed reached clarity? What? What?*

Why do people want to think when they run? It goes wrong. Thinking always goes wrong.

Speaking of thinking, think about this: I stop, finally, to catch my breath and I immediately start panicking that I am going to seize up and never, ever, get home. While I am doing this, though, I notice something peculiar.

We are at the foot of a tower crane. There is a man standing there with a video camera. The crane is moving in its slow, graceful manner, taking hold of things that are at rest far below the cabin in which the driver sits and moving them from one place to the other. I always love watching cranes. And then my favourite bit happens.

It is the changing of the guard. One man is ascending the narrow ladders within the mast of the crane. The current driver has stopped his work and waits for his replacement. I assume that the cabin cannot be left unoccupied while the crane is switched on so he has to wait until the new guy has got all the way to the top. I do not know for sure if this is true, but it feels like it may be the case.

I look at the cameraman and wonder if he holds some sort of surveillance role. He is wearing a hi-vis jacket. I don't want to talk to him but decide that I must. Curiosity gets the better of me.

When I walk towards him I hear that he is speaking. He is muttering to himself. He is saying 'fall, come on, fall, go on, fall' under his breath.

I ask him why he wants the men on the tower crane to fall – what he possibly has to gain from such a thing happening. He tells me that if somebody falls, and he catches it on camera, he can finally leave, submit what he has filmed – whatever that means – and move on to the next job. Move on to another tall structure, and that he will finally be relieved of the pressure he is under to provide.

I leave and start jogging in the direction of home, once again thinking, with every step, how much I wish I was doing something else. *I wish I had to stand around filming cranes. At least then I could stand still. At least then I wouldn't have to be fucking jogging.* And then, finally, I seem to go brain dead until I find myself in the shower, aching, but strangely feeling good about myself. Maybe that is why they do it, after all.

Nondescript persons on the bridge

They were stood on a bridge. The woman was holding a camera and pointing it at her husband.

"Stop squinting while I try and take the photo. It makes you look more short-sighted than you actually are."

"I'm trying to identify that person behind you. That person who has been behind you for the past few days, intermittently."

"What are you talking about?"

"I'm talking about that person who has been behind you for the past few days, intermittently."

"As in you're talking intermittently, or are you telling me that the person has been behind me intermittently?"

"Well, both, but if you didn't interrupt me and make me repeat myself then just the latter."

"Alright, cleverdick."

"Hmmm."

"Look at the camera. This is for the cover or the jacket or whatever it's called."

"Dust cover?"

Somebody else: "Or dust jacket."

"Thanks", they both said to the informative passerby who happened to be at the right place at the right time. He nodded and smiled and cycled on.

"Okay, look at this one," the woman said.

"It's okay, but I'm squinting in it."

"Hmmm."

"Shouldn't we both be in it?"

"One each, I reckon."

"That much space?"

"Maybe."

"I want to talk about that person who's been behind you, intermittently, for the past few days."

"Yes."

"I'm going to keep mentioning her until you look."

She turned round and looked at the person.

"I see her. I recognise her, sort of vaguely; possibly because she looks like everybody else I've ever seen."

"Possibly."

"She's nondescript. How do you know she's been there, intermittently, for the past few days?"

"I have a keen eye for full fringes."

"That's not a full fringe."

"Well, whatever it is."

"It doesn't matter."

"That man on the bicycle was good looking."

"Was he?"

"Yes."

"I didn't look at him, although I did appreciate his bibliophilic input."

"He looked like nearly every other man on a bike."

"Hardcore or midlife?"

"The other one, actually."

"What, trying to make an I've-not-got-a-car point?"

"Yes. Beard."

"Hemp satchel?"

"No."

"Defiance personified."

"I just took another one of you while you looked down and smirked. Do you like it?"

"It's similar to the first."

"But more natural."

"Hmmm."

" ..."

" ..."

"I'd not mention that woman, if you can help it. Just for a while," said the woman.

"Just to pretend our minds are at rest."

" ..."

" ..."

Simultaneous nodding. They turned and walked back the way they had come along the opaque canal.

<u>I'm So Happy That You Actually Came Out To See Me Despite The Fact That I Can Taste The Bad Taste That You Can Taste In Your Mouth Whenever You Think About Me (or I.S.H.T.Y.A.C.O.T.S.M.D.T .F.T.I.C.T.T.B.T.T.Y.C.T.I.Y.M.W.Y.T.A.M. for short).</u>

"I feel weak."

    "We shouldn't be doing this. Not this openly."

    "I feel susceptible to anything."

    "..."

    "I accidentally did something yesterday that I hate myself for doing."

    "..."

    "Do you think it's possible that I unwittingly do things that other people want? Do you think it's possible that everything is just a big network of interconnected things that all point in one direction? All insinuate a certain message and get you to behave in a certain way, regardless of whether you actually want to?"

    "..."

    "Or do you think I'm just paranoid? Solipsistic? That I just see things as connected because I'm operating a one-track mind that picks up on certain things and interprets them in a certain way?"

    "..."

    "I mean, come on, it's not like all these things, all these people, are concerned with me, is it?"

    "..."

    "I'm seeing links between unconnected things."

240

"…"

"I'm seeing things I think I've seen before and not recognising things I used to think I knew well."

"…"

"So I guess that means I don't know them that well."

"…"

I hold her stare for a few seconds and hope that nobody can see that we're doing this. Isn't hanging about with your fellow jurors a criminal offence? People seem to be watching. Olwyn is so boring. She bored me in the bathroom and now she's boring me here.

"What are you doing? Wait, don't... why... are you doing that?"

"…"

"You'll get bean juice all in your hair and on your smart clothes."

"…"

"Can you still hear me?"

"…"

"Well I guess your ears are not submerged."

"…"

"Nod if you are still listening. Or wiggle your shoulders or something."

I let out a groan, into my beans on toast.

"I'll take that as a yes then, if you don't mind."

"…"

"An answer in the affirmative, so to speak."

"…"

241

"Do you get my drift?"

"..."

"Anyway, as I was saying, it's not like all these people I've started noticing have ever crossed paths with me before, never mind care about me or anything that I do."

Fuck me. Isn't everything just meaningless, anyway? Must everything be linked?

"People look so similar these days. I think I'm just being paranoid."

"..."

"Nothing happens for a reason, if you see where I'm coming from."

"..."

"Does that make me a nihilist? I used to want to be one of those when I grew up."

Nihilist/healer. Puh-tay-tow/puh-tay-tow. The plate hurts my nose.

"Small world, if you, like, know what I mean, or something."

"..."

"It's interesting though, isn't it? How these things can all seem related. How you get something in your head and let it bounce around and then something else comes along and you let it get merged in with your initial concern, somehow. Like snowballing worry."

"..."

"A network of sadness. Of related worry."

"..."

"I quite like that. Do you think it works?"

"..."

"I might write it down or something. Might write a poem in my lunch break."

"..."

"In my lunch break. Tomorrow."

"..."

"This lunch break is nearly up now, by the way."

"..."

"Are you going to eat that, or just sit there with your face in it?"

Is it genuinely possible to be bored to death? I can feel myself slipping away.

"Five minutes. You probably need to wash your face."

Nope, that's me done.

"Seriously. If we both show up late we'll get rumbled and our little chats are the kind of thing that can get you in a lot of trouble."

"..."

"Right, this isn't that funny really. I was humouring you at first but now..."

"..."

"Move. Now."

"..."

"Come on, Theresa, move."

I'm fading, but I can just about feel a small flag mounted on a cocktail stick fall out of my hair and land next to my submerged face.

"Are you okay?"

"…"

"Wait, shit, are you actually okay?"

"…"

"Fuck, are you okay?"

"…"

"Fuck. Oh shit."

I vaguely feel somebody shaking my arm. I don't bother holding on. It is done.

"…"

"Oh no. Help."

"…"

"Excuse me, with the phone. Yes, sorry, please could you call an ambulance?"

A Fish & Chip Shop

They opened up around five p.m. on an evening
a few weeks after their first opening. The evening
looked like it was never really going to properly get
started nor end. It was going to stagnate, this evening.
Already established as a semi-regular occurrence in
their sapling catering careers, they liked to call this
feeling 'perpetual teatime'. And although, if it was
accepted as existent by anybody else – which it only
very occasionally was – such a phenomenon was
good for business, it was bad for morale. Some of
the evening's customers would become deluded –
convinced by their malfunctioning body clocks – that
they had not yet eaten, would have the bright idea
of going for a Friday night chippy that they did not
realise they had just thrown the leftovers of into the
bin, and schlep back out and purchase exactly the
same order again. Sometimes, if the phenomenon
was taking place with utmost vitality, the people
would actually walk backwards from their house
after they had just finished their first meal, like they
were actually being rewound, purchase their chips
and then throw themselves into gear and head
home, facing the usual direction. Certain people
got stuck in this loop all night until the shop ran
out of chips. Then they walked home, through the
breaking dawn, disgruntled that they had not yet
managed to have their evening meal. In spite of the
fact that they had overeaten to the point of vomiting

three times and nearly shat themselves on their sixth backwards walk to the chip shop in as many hours.

On such evenings hands would tire and an otherwise solid marriage would bear the strains of time malfunctioning and things would be all-round bad in general. As if to make this point, a greased-up wedding ring fell from an ill-advisedly gloveless extremity into the vat, followed by an instinctive hand trying to fish it out, followed by the transformation of an already bad mood into a gruesome one, the hand's owner standing by the cold tap for more than an hour, getting wrinkles to compliment the blisters. She told him to make himself useful and start on the fish.

People came in dribs and drabs. Lots of the usuals, along with a group of fourteen or so who claimed to be the inaugural Manchester City fourteen-man football team.

When they first opened the chip shop they had decided to place a black book on a small table in the area of the shop where the customers waited for – and often, when it was rainy, ate – whatever it was that they bought. In this book they had decided to ask people to write down their answers to certain questions. This was the means by which they would collect the necessary data for their project, which they, after much arguing, had decided to call '*Gastronomic Routine and the Tall Orders of Societal Expectation: an exploratory glance at how personality is reflected in the eating habits of everybody who can afford to*

246

have them', which they felt would satisfy the needs of their employer. A continuation of their heretofore unsuccessful 'undercover academia' project, sort of. But they wouldn't mention that. Once collected, they would write the definitive work on their chosen issue, and, although it could be deemed selling out given their employer, build their career from there. What avenue such a book would lead them down was uncertain but they were not sure if they really cared. The reality was that any reality was better than their recent reality: teaching for slippery wages and little hope that anything would follow. So when the call had come the attitude had been something of a mix-up between 'thank fuck' and 'fuck it'. In the black book the members of the fourteen-man football team had not answered the questions. They had simply signed their names and numbers, one to fourteen, scattered out of order down the page, in a formation indicating their supposed positions.

The shop was starting to get busy: people were streaming in just as the remaining few from the first sporadic serving session had brought themselves back to the counter for an unwitting round two. Thankfully the fourteen-man football team did not appear to be susceptible to perpetual teatime. The crowd was the usual, given their moderately sized circle of friends in the field, and consequently the place became tweedier and bookier as perpetual teatime crawled on. They wondered how long this support from their friends would last. How long it would be until they just drew the normal sort of people you find at chip shops: people who come in, order, stop at longest for the amount of time it takes to eat, and then leave. Rather than hanging about all night talking, being well-meaning, believing that by making the place look busier, it made people passing by think it must be really good, tempting them to come in and try. They weren't sure they liked this overwhelming presence that filled the shop at the moment. Yes, they were seeking to discuss things – verbally and in a written sense via the black book – in which this sort of clientele possessed expertise. However, it hardly did wonders for their demographic range, nor for providing insight into the minds of those unfamiliar with the material they often asked about. Perhaps they ought to de-intellectualise a little. Ask more mundane questions. Try not to scare people off. Tonight the questions were picked. But tomorrow things could change. Put the early wrong-footing down to inexperience. And the odd bit of highbrow was okay, just as long as it was interspersed with other things. The woman started to talk to people, commanding the room whether people liked it or not, always performing, as was natural to her – almost certainly a habit that could be attributed to too long in a certain profession.

A customer walked in. She was drunk. She went up to the counter and ordered something and the woman started talking to her. The woman looked for the black book out amongst the hubbub of hungry patrons and, upon turning to the man to ask where it was, noticed that he was standing next to it. The woman told him to listen and take notes and proceeded to ask the customer a few of the exploratory questions they had decided upon whilst setting up shop. The man wrote tenderly, with the hand wet from its time under the tap dripping onto the page and causing the ink to smudge a little.

The customer left with her chips, swaying, and the evening carried on feeling like it was not progressing.

X2

"I don't think it is possible to ever grow out of pre-meeting nerves," the woman said, as they walked off the bus and made their way to an arranged location.

The decision to have this meeting had been made the night beforehand. It was the result of a late night phone call from a stranger offering them some sort of commission, as in, actually offering them money in return for writing something. Desperation, as it often did, had clouded any sort of serious consideration of the usual dangers associated with the arrangement of meetings in industrial estates at the behest of strangers claiming to have money until it was almost too late. The eventual consideration of such things meant that the man now carried a bread knife – still in its Everyday Value wrapping – in the inside pocket of his sheepskin coat.

The bus had taken an hour and the traffic hadn't even been that bad. They had got out of work over at the university on Oxford Road quite a while ago now, and had yet to allow themselves to wind down and settle into any sort of weekend mentality. Whatever the outcome of this meeting, the pair of them had agreed that it was likely to change things significantly.

The knife was slightly too long for its pocket and the handle pressed against the man's armpit as he walked. He complained about this to the woman, who ignored him and moved slightly ahead so as to avoid the awkward swinging of the arm as the man repeatedly tried to adjust the way he walked to accommodate for his load without revealing it. The way he looked was important today, he thought. The woman took off her scarf and shoved it into her pocket, deciding that the less there was on her that was grabbable the better. Neither wanted to admit it, but both felt that they were more nervous than the other, and both were embarrassed by this.

They rounded a corner and found themselves staring at the place that they assumed that they were supposed to enter. It loomed. Through a large set of gates, under a red-and-white maximum height sign and towards a set of doors marked reception; the couple started to wonder if they were being asked to write some sort of instruction manual or something. They had no idea what it was that this factory produced.

The receptionist's synthetic beehive was resting at a jaunty angle on her head, threatening to fall. She was picking her teeth with a cocktail stick with a flag on the end of it and, as they entered, she slowly allowed her eyelids to open and rolled her eyes upwards in their direction, taking a number of seconds to do all of this. It was clearly a rehearsed thing. 'What?' was asked and they spoke the name of the person they had been told to come and meet. They were told to wait five minutes, which they did, and were then led, by a man in hi-vis, down a totally blank corridor and told to sit in a room that looked suspiciously like the one they had just been in, minus the receptionist. The hi-vis man handed them a pile of magazines that they had not seen him carrying and told them to make themselves at home. He then left.

The man placed the pile of magazines onto the floor and stood on them, elevating himself to a level at which he could see out of a tiny window set into the wall up near the ceiling. The woman asked him why he hadn't just stood on a chair. The man got down off the magazine pile and dragged a chair over to the window, stood on it and looked out. On the other side of the window was an office, of sorts. It was sparsely furnished, the floor uncarpeted and the floorboards untreated. In the centre of the office was a large wingback chair and in front of that was a low card table. The only light in the room was that passing through the window through which the man was looking. He could make out the silhouette of a large standard lamp behind the wingback chair.

The door behind them opened and the man jumped, so much so that he stumbled off the chair and landed, having done a short twist mid-air, facing a large man in a red suit. The large man was rubbing Brylcream into his hair, and didn't stop walking, knocking the man down as he made his way past them and entered the room that contained the wingback chair, closing the door behind him.

Ten minutes later, after the man had got back up again and dusted himself off, there was a shout from the room and the door opened, seemingly of its own accord. The man and woman walked through it and heard it shut behind them. The man noticed that the standard lamp was now on, and that it was fitted with a blue bulb. On the card table sat a brightly coloured box that they both immediately recognised and next to it there was a small orange plastic packet. The woman gave the man a look and they both started to feel that this could all start to work out rather well for them. At least they now had an idea of the sort of power they were dealing with. The large man, who was seated in the wingback chair, smiled up at them and invited them to sit down. There were no other seats in the room, so they sat on the floor. The large man looked down at them from his position in the chair and asked them what they were doing. He reiterated his command for them to sit down, and this time patted both of his knees as he did so. The couple looked at each other, thought about their day jobs, and obeyed.

They then proceeded to have the most intimate and potentially productive meeting of their lives. Two hours later they left the unusual office with the keys to a retail unit and an envelope containing more money than they had ever held.

Mr E. C. S

About midway through university I made a friend called Alan who was from an area near to where I resided out of term time. We met through a mutual friend called Lotte, from Crawley, whom I had first met during a university library induction and Alan had apparently met on some sort of social event for people interested in musical theatre. For a year or so Alan and I went on being friends of Lotte's without meeting one another. I never really heard about him from Lotte, either. Early on in our university careers Lotte and I had independently flirted with the idea of becoming some sort of item, although by the time either of us knew that the other had done this as well things had progressed between Lotte and Alan to the point where it would seem like I was doing something out of order, although it wasn't like Lotte and Alan were together or anything. Anyway, it was because Lotte and Alan were not really together or anything that Alan and I started to spend time together.

Naturally, because it transpired that we lived so close to one another when we were back home, Alan and I made an effort to keep in contact over the holidays. I didn't really introduce him to my home friends much; Alan was the sort of person who liked to think he was a leader, not a joiner, so bringing him into large preformed groups didn't really work. He preferred to meet people in ones and twos and build what was, in his mind, a group that revolved around him. Where he was the glue.

One of his ways of making people aware that he was in charge was to give out nicknames. The usual sort of logic – once you have named somebody, you sort of have a strange kind of authority over them. You established a part of their public identity, so you are almost automatically on a level above them: that of the creator rather than the created. Only in a small kind of way, but nevertheless Alan took this belief of his very seriously. Problem was, he was terrible at coming up with nicknames that would stick. In the end he resorted to using my middle name – which my parents chose, thus undermining the whole point – and called me Caleb. Though I did overhear him occasionally claiming that he came up with it in some sort of (he thought) clever reference to my Jewish roots that he'd obviously researched for some time after he had started calling me Caleb. Embarrassing, right.

Anyway, the reason I'm thinking about Alan is because I'm up here on my own, having given up on my plan to try and be ordinary about a week ago. Instead I decided to follow my followers. Which brought me here. And when alone I tend to reminisce.

One summer, Lotte decided to catch the train up north and come and visit Alan and I in our homeland. Alan was working a summer job, and this was around the time – just as we were about to start the dreaded final year, on the precipice of reality – that I was panicking about being alone and started to re-entertain the deluded idea of trying to make something with Lotte. Ridiculous I know, and had I ever tried she'd have had the sense to tell me to come off it. But sometimes we all get a little self-absorbed and sit on the bus looking morosely out of the window, embodying a cliché that should never have come into existence in the first place. So I found myself entertaining the idea, and in turn resenting the fact that she might prefer other people to me. Bear with me. This is all relevant. The reason that I mention that I was in such a stupid state of mind is because that laid the foundations for my pathetic behaviour that followed. I became increasingly irritable as I grew paranoid that, as the days wore on during the time Lotte was visiting, and we killed time in the park and at the pub and on the moors, she was waiting, tolerating me, until Alan arrived on the scene. Looking back, she did nothing to give me this idea. I did it all by myself. So I was at first angry, and then became resigned to my self-appointed status as placeholder, and then started to go into autopilot, repaying Lotte for what I thought she was doing by trying to be equally uninterested in her. Wow, you must be feeling really sorry for me right now. Naturally, this pissed her off, relations soured, and after a slightly forced third year of friendship, we pretty much severed contact after congratulating one another on our irritatingly high two-ones.

I've been thinking that it's awful how I can just walk away – just lose people and things – with such efficiency as soon as I become obsessed with an idea or myself. Maybe it's natural. Inherent even. Does everybody make everything about themselves in their own mind as soon as they fear everything is not about themselves in the minds of others? I realised I had this habit when I was trying to be boring, and had the time to think. These past months I became obsessed with this following thing and barely spoke to my band; my real friends; my family. Not thinking for a moment what other people may be doing because I am focused only on myself and those I have decided are obsessed with me. And I think, as things progress in, like, a universal sort of way, everybody will start to be increasingly like this. They too will focus only on their own ideas; absorbed by perceptions of themselves. It's like I've arrived early to a point of disconnection. That I've fast-forwarded through the good bits and arrived at the end already, where all I can do is stop and watch all the nastiness in store for other people play out as they catch up to where I am.

So here I am, in the cold, on top of this multistorey car park, still involved. Here because I am, finally, not leading people to places. They led me here. Well, sort of indirectly, via the all-knowing Ralph. And I got here before them, which goes a fair way towards contradicting my status as the follower. But I am only here because I know they have already made the decision to come here, and will do so sooner or later. Anyway, I don't know how Ralph knew to send me here. I can't figure it out, so I won't try to explain.

Perhaps he was right after all. They can't follow me if I am following them, surely. Where would we end up then?

It's freezing. I've been here ages. Two days, wrapped from the nipples down in a sleeping bag and sat on a deck chair, drinking tins and chain smoking, waiting for them to arrive. In an attempt to prevent any sort of circulatory issues I'm bobbing up and down, flapping my arms which are extended out to my sides. Weirdly, my surroundings seem to be doing the same thing. Moving up and down – it feels so fast that it's like a blur. I've finally put a stop to it. No more acceleration. No more hurtling to conclusion. We're paused. Blur away, if that's the confirmation.

They arrived about five minutes ago. I do not know what they are doing, but I know that they think that they are not being watched. This is a weird feeling. The spectator. For so long I've felt like I've been under scrutiny.

They climb with what looks like skill. I assume that they have done this before. Looks good. Might give it a go myself, my now slightly pissed mind tells me. But I could never do it.

As the pair of them rest about half way up I duck

behind the perimeter wall of the car park and crack open another can. I know they must be looking around, admiring the view. And who knows what sort of night vision abilities they might possess? The beer hisses as it opens and I wonder how far the sound carries across the night. I hope that the owner of the car that has been parked beside me for the past three days does not return tonight, of all nights. I need a shower. I need a shave. I shamefacedly look over to the corner of the car park where I last shat and pissed into a discarded cardboard box. I daren't return to the scene of the crime for fear of rain-induced disintegration of the papery structure. I light another one and cough. I feel my eye twitch. I peek over the top of the waist-high wall and notice that the couple have started to ascend again, going a little slower this time around. Nevertheless, it is still impressive to watch them as they leap from one girder to another displaying upper body strength that I could only ever achieve if I brought to a skidding, grinding halt my alarmingly swift acquisition of breasts and belly. Not too bad now, but apparently these things accelerate remarkably. I study my yellowish nails with disgust and wish I'd brought easy-peel satsumas. Satsumas are all I've been eating during this little holiday of mine. Talk about on a shoestring.

They are still climbing. I think it is the woman who is slightly ahead of the man.

The other day Ralph was talking to me about a

friend of his – one of Ralph's more unusual friends, I gather, although Ralph would not disclose exactly who it was. I don't know if it is somebody I have met or not.

Ralph was telling me that this friend was busy having something of a crisis the last time he visited. The problem that this friend highlighted was that he had a classic case of the old 'Reviewers' Paradox'. That was what Ralph called it. He got his kicks out of getting rid of things he hated. Of cleaning up. Out of ruthless anti-pontification. A man of action, apparently this guy lived to get rid of what was not necessary. What he felt did not contribute sufficiently to whatever it was that he felt that he was protecting. Society, or whatever else it may have been. He really got off over that sort of thing, apparently. He exercised this life-giving occupation of his through making these elements of society victims of their own supposed faults. For example, he offered vast sums of money to bad music journalists in return for them attempting to review their own record reviews; supposedly for some sort of meta-literary magazine he had dreamt up as a cover story. The ideal result would be the bad journalist became locked in a paradox of informing themselves, through writing a (supposedly inarticulate) review, that they were not very good at writing reviews. This was what Ralph said, although I must say I find it a bit baffling, as it seems to require the sudden acquisition of a remarkable amount of self-awareness from somebody initially chosen because of their lack of such a virtue. Anyway, the friend's problem was that if he was perfectly efficient and successful in his quest then he would lose all the materials necessary to continue in it. I understand that I may have confused this with my use of another sort of Reviewer's Paradox in the example, but what I think Ralph means by Reviewers' Paradox is that the situation his friend is in resembles that of somebody who makes a living out of slagging things off, thus potentially jeopardising the careers and the continuation of those people and things he relies upon in order to make his living. You can't be a harsh reviewer when there is nothing to review.

What I'm getting at, I think, is that part of me, niggling, almost subconscious but obviously not, is worried that if I've put a stop to this paranoid obsession I may no longer have anything to completely occupy me. Yes, I have shaken something that I perceive to be bad. But in a world so preoccupied with complaint, what does one do if they have nothing to moan about? Is it wise to wantonly eliminate my most noteworthy gripe? I know that this obsession feeds my nasty habit of abandoning people. I know I need to re-assimilate with the important aspects of my day-to-day life. But at the same time I'm terrified of boredom. I don't know what I want, and neither does anybody else.

These exceptional guys know what they want, though. They are now standing on the uppermost part of the big wheel. The view must be miraculous. I am now looking up at them, the car park in which I sit being, by the usual standards, pretty squat.

I don't think I've ever seen anybody die before.

My personal favourite flight path was that of the woman: uninterrupted. I couldn't handle the reality of the man's. I was sick.

JEN-EE

Jenny had joined the Manchester division of the Amateur Rooftop Sightseeing and Exploration Society. She was busy distracting herself with her newfound hobby when she encountered something that left her shaken.

Her new hobby disappointed her. She did not see the point in joining a society that sent you off, with a camera, on your own. She was to report back to headquarters with photos and plotted coordinates, thus aiding the society's ultimate and unfathomable goal of charting all of Manchester's rooftops. The group's headquarters was a double-parked motorhome filled with cartography equipment over by Victoria Station, manned only by slightly creepy Graham, who occupied the whole breadth of all kinds of spectrums.

Having been a member for only a few days, Jenny was given the boring jobs – the multistorey car parks, the rooftop bars, any houses that would happily let her in. She had to be at least what Graham called 'level three' before she was trusted to take part in any of the operations that involved breaking and entering – and also involved working in teams – and so Jenny was stuck strolling around on her own, like she was on some sort of antisocial beat patrol, until Graham deemed her contribution valuable enough to justify moving her up a level. The levels were, of course, entirely of Graham's discretion. Jenny had only joined because, of all the societies advertised in the newspaper, this was the only one that required subs that amounted to less than fifty pounds. A one-off payment of forty-three quid. Which Graham stuck in his back pocket and presumably spent on some sort of niche sex.

All of this was in aid of what Jenny thought of as her social CV. It wasn't that she didn't have any friends. It was just that they were all mature and settled and proper. They actually had things to talk about that didn't make them seem like obsessives or addicts or pervs or failures. Jenny was, despite herself, becoming a wallflower in her middle age. And so she was actively trying to fulfil two needs with these recent forays into niche pastimes: find new friends, and find hobbies to exaggerate and waffle on about to the friends she already had. Her logic was that the weirder hobbies would attract the weirder people and thus, at least in the ideal scenario, the genuinely interesting ones. Jenny knew it didn't always work like that. But joining these groups had already worked in one case. She had Theresa now, didn't she?

She walked up the final ramp in the car park, which was situated directly opposite another – her next target – and between the two stood a monstrous white circle, made of girders. Jenny hated it. It wanted to be London. Touristy. Unnecessary. What you needed to see you could see without paying, if you were smart. Jenny had just managed that.

Where she stood was level with the wheel's highest point, and she'd burned through calories to get there. It stood there looking at her and she was looking at it.

And she was not the only one. There was a throng of people at the top of the car park. Weird. Jenny put on her glasses and took a closer look. Fuck. He was there. The multi-loving Guy, or whatever it was he claimed to be. Member of the congregation of crazy from the other week. 'Are you a walker or in a band' Guy, or whatever it was that he said. Rainbow wotsits with the tuba. Twat. Giving her leaflets and all that. He was wearing a T-shirt emblazoned with a string of letters that didn't seem to make any sense, and was setting out chairs in rows which were being quickly occupied by people wearing T-shirts similar to the man's, only in a variety of colours, all available for 'only four pounds fifty' from a stand over near the edge of the roof. This seemed to be quite a spectacle they were expecting. Jenny forgot about her camera and moved into the shadows to watch the situation unfold. The Guy who Jenny kept seeing, and who was obviously in charge of this situation, finished putting out the chairs and started to circulate, answering questions that Jenny could not hear and generally making everybody feel welcome, which was obvious to Jenny as the muscles in their faces visibly relaxed from a position which collectively betrayed extreme anxiety and uncertainty and became examples of the elusive-unless-in-marketing concept of the 'dentist's smile'. Jenny's dentist always had bad breath so she made it one of her tactical quirks to offer him mints whenever they met. She would pass him boxes and he would guzzle them with his blackening teeth – perhaps a similar phenomenon to the one involving many chefs eating badly – mistakenly reading it as a sign that Jenny was flirting with him. Playing the long game, he must assume, after ten years of routinely and platonically monitoring her oral hygiene.

The Guy was slowly making his way to the front of the little viewing theatre he had created – facing the big circle – smiling at people and passing out what looked like mega-size tissues upon request. When he got to the front of the congregation he began to gesticulate and talk in a raised voice, so Jenny could hear what he was saying.

He was saying things about this being the first time this had been done in a live setting. He urged them all to relax and treat it as normal, because everybody was equally nervous and equally inexperienced and everybody was in the same boat with regards to wanting to feel comfortable in their surroundings. He gestured at the big wheel again.

Everybody's eyes were on the wheel rather than the Guy who was speaking. The Guy started talking about how he wanted to construct an environment where people could experience pure, unadulterated, wrongfully tabooed human feeling that was too often obstructed by modern, pristine ideology that dictated everybody behaved in a certain way and considered certain things unacceptable. He said that the situation that all of the attendees were in was a secret one and a beneficial one. That there was nothing wrong with them for wanting to do this. He asked if everybody was sitting comfortably, and said that he had it on good authority that what they were there to see would most likely happen that night. But if not, get to know one another. Make a sleepover out of it. Or something ridiculous like that. They had a *multitude* of refreshments, apparently.

He said again that the taboo thing they were about to enjoy was perfectly fine, and that he had been experiencing it in a pure and unadulterated way for a number of years. Albeit not live, as this was the first time that had been done. He said it was remarkable that such a debut would take place at this scale, and attract this level of interest. It was unprecedented, he said, even though he claimed he had always somehow known. But anyway, he had done it before and he was completely fine. Good, even. He ended with something about experiencing life. About how activities like these were painfully finite when they were conducted most efficiently, and so they must be enjoyed 'to the core'. He said 'to the core'.

The Guy turned and theatrically gasped. He reached down and picked up a large placard on which was written, in black marker pen, 'the time has come'. Jenny could just about make out two specks circling the wheel's base.

They were too far away for Jenny to make them out in any great detail. As far as she was aware, as she gazed from her hiding place trying to get a good view despite numerous obstructions, the specks were two people down on the ground. The one in the lead started to climb the structure. The other one followed, only slightly behind. They made their way upwards – at a reasonable pace – approaching Jenny's eye level, and she was able to strain a little less in order to see. Jenny looked back at the people assembled in their chairs on the roof. They were all watching intently, through small viewfinder type things, like the ones you get in theatres to aid those watching from the seats on the balcony. Jenny was not so fortunate as to have access to such a tool. Wanting to keep the congregation in view as much as she did the spectacle – so that she could watch them experience this intense, taboo pleasure the Guy had been speaking about – Jenny stayed put, thinking she might go over to the edge once the two climbers got higher.

She looked again at the crowd of people. The Guy was sat at the front, in a chair he placed right in the middle of his seating arrangement. Then she noticed something disturbing. When the Guy lifted up a ringed finger everybody in the gathering made adjustments to their clothing. With the hand not occupied with the holding of the binocular things they all started to get busy in one way or another, some tentative at first, some going with gusto, attempting to defy embarrassment with enthusiasm. Jenny decided that she was definitely now more interested in the spectacle than the reaction, and moved slowly towards the edge of the car park, staying amongst the shadows cast onto her side by a neighbouring office block – although she doubted that anybody was really looking anywhere but through their binoculars. This was a situation. Jenny wondered what this taboo pleasure usually forbidden was going to turn out to be. What was it that they evidently liked so much? Was this some sort of communal display of free-climbing fetishes? At the edge of the rooftop Jenny was able to poke her head over the wall and look down at the people as they travelled upwards, towards her. Somebody behind her moaned and Jenny assumed that this meant that they were out of whatever game it was that they were playing. Rustling of tissue and whispered commiserations bounced off the walls alarmingly – percussive accompaniment to an otherwise totally silent night. Until you noticed the cars. And the hum. And the quiet purring of people really getting into the groove of things back there. And the irritatingly loud buzz of Jenny's phone, which she had thought that she had turned off. Fuck. It was Graham, asking her what was taking so long, no doubt. Jenny wondered what the cartographic symbol for premeditated communal masturbation was. She took out her piece of paper and sketched the area, roughly, and populated it with an exclamation mark and a picture of a stickman doing whatever with *was that one of his legs?* She didn't answer the phone for fear that people would notice her, and quickly sent a text to the caller to vaguely suggest she was okay but in the middle of something.

The climbers had been stationary on one of the pods about half way up for the past few minutes. They came close to one another – perhaps searching through a pocket or something, and then separated slightly. Jenny could still not make them out particularly well. They began to ascend again. As they climbed up they moved around the structure so that they were as far away from Jenny as they could be. Faces obstructed by the thick white spokes and blurred by what seemed unfeasible speed, they made their way up past the level from which Jenny was watching them – without noticing their audience – and came to a second stop at the highest point, facing away from Jenny, towards the multistorey opposite. They were interacting with one another again. Pointing, maybe speaking. They looked intimate and Jenny felt strangely comforted by this. The darkness – their position on the wheel being above the reach of the street lamps – made it hard to make out more than shapes. Just nondescript human figures.

She couldn't figure out why, but Jenny expected it when they jumped. The people behind her got excited. She just watched, two figures approaching the webbed shadow that decorated the floor far

270

below, falling hand in hand at first. She watched their backs fall away from her. She felt like she had seen this all before. It felt trivial, like it had been served to her in a way that meant she ought to assume that it didn't matter. Then grace was ruined and the structure got in the way of one. Moments separated what Jenny assumed was the certain termination of each life. Jenny looked away as people behind her whooped and one confused guy seemed to ask for it all one more time. She glanced back at the group and realised that a small proportion were leaving, hurriedly, not looking back. The Guy was standing, bowing, as if this was all some sort of grand performance he'd directed.

Jenny wondered about calling somebody but didn't. She made sure that the Guy was still facing his dwindling crowd – a crowd torn between elation and shock; some more torn than others – and that he had their undivided attention. Then she walked towards the rusting green fire escape in the corner and began the long, plodding descent. Step by step she made her way down to the level of the deceased climbers. She wondered who would clean all this up. She wondered if any of her old friends were awake. She thought about ringing her dad.

Once on the ground Jenny did not walk towards the square where she knew she would find two people. Instead she resolved to spend the rest of the night alone. Maybe she'd collar a street sweeper if she passed one on her way. She could tell them

271

that there was some serious mess that they probably didn't deserve to have to clean up.

But they would be there, and sometimes that was all somebody needed to be to become implicated. There and dirty and living.